A Sin to Forgive

Daniel Dydek

BEORN

BEORN PUBLISHING, LLC

Contents

Chapter 1

I cannot help, now, but to be in grateful awe of Our Father's blessed timing. Looking back over our journeys I see clearly the ebb and flow, from rest to tremendous external pressures. From delights to terrors that frayed every nerve. Without those ebbs, the flows would surely have undone us.

But in the months after we defeated the dragon, I worried that Thomas and I spent a long and too-luxurious winter at Fosse. The table set by the Pendrels never wavered in meats or conversations, now they had been freed from the dragon and its curses. We made many friends, passed away many an hour in pleasantries or past-times. Occasionally Lord Pendrel would call for Thomas or me—or both—to attend a meeting or judgement. Not so often his own rule would erode, or his people's faith in his abilities, but especially when he perceived Our Father might have particular wisdom.

The snows left the valley first, but Lord Pendrel prevailed upon us to remain until the passes were clearer. And while I was not restless in spirit or in the Sacred Fire, I began to feel it in my mind and legs.

Finally, as we broke fast one day, Lord Pendrel informed us the roads would be open—that he had a particular convoy heading south anyway if we cared to join it. I remembered Aurden, how I had felt eager for the next challenge and what had come of it. I glanced at Thomas first to read his expression. He smiled at me as if he knew, and I lowered my eyes.

"Of course, my Lord," I replied. "I fear we must."

Both Lord and Lady smiled upon us. "Perhaps you will not say it aloud," his Lordship said. "But we thank you for the unspoken compliment, over and above everything else for which we owe you thanks."

"You have amply repaid all," I responded. "Through your care, attention, and honor. I feel..." I paused, realizing the truth as I spoke it. "I feel well-rested for our next duty."

Near the end of the hall, Mahmoud eyed me and frowned just slightly. What could I say to him? He should be used to it by now.

It took us less than a week before a final ridge-top gave us a view of the broad sea, gray now in early spring. Mahmoud told us it was nearly blue in summer. He said it in troubled tones. I glanced at him curiously.

"Do you expect a hard voyage?" I asked.

His glance flickered. "With you, I always expect some trouble."

I smiled gently. "It was only for a few weeks this time," I said. "And remember, you missed Aurden."

He inclined his head, and we rode on silently.

Thomas touched my arm, drawing me back as we let the convoy go a little ahead. "Do *you* expect a hard voyage?" he asked me.

I focused on the Flame, lost for a moment in its flickering. When I came back to myself, the port loomed ahead and the sun was nearly set. "We will make it to the other side," I said simply. I looked at

Thomas and allowed myself a short sigh. "I suppose that's all we can ask for."

He glanced at me, waggled his eyebrows. I grinned sheepishly and looped my fingers through his.

And prayed for strength.

Mahmoud led us along the wharf—the rest of the convoy was only coming to port, not to cross the sea—inquiring at several of the ships. Most were not sailing for a month or more. "Are we in a hurry?" I asked after the fourth.

He peered at me a moment. "No, and yes," was all he said. His mule seemed used to it, and plodded steadily behind him.

We stopped at the fifth. "Port of Algiers?" he asked, not expecting a different answer.

"Tomorrow," the mate responded. He glanced at the sky, then aboard. "We're nearly full, and Captain wants to be off."

Mahmoud looked at us as though for approval. Thomas shrugged at me, and I shrugged back. I no longer felt like waiting would change much.

A crewman was called to help unload the mule, and Thomas helped as well. While the men worked, I glanced around the dock. A hawk-nosed man with a long but cheerful enough face lounged across the way, watching the proceedings. Black hair hung lank on his shoulders. I could not tell his profession, though he twirled a coin across slender, nimble fingers.

He was not the only one on the dock; as my gaze swept across, I counted three others who looked to be waiting to board as well. One I would have placed in a monastery, though he lacked the tonsure and brown robes. Another looked like a merchant with a dark beard well-trimmed and oiled, wearing a bright vest over his dark blue tunic. The third matched Mahmoud, perhaps more strictly dressed in Saracen attire.

I heard Thomas' boots approaching, but before I turned I saw, nestled among a pile of crates and baskets, a pair of red glowing eyes, burning steadily at me. The Fire rose a notch—though not in alarm. The eyes never blinked, and I felt with a shudder as though it was studying me.

Not more rats. But these eyes, when they finally departed, lowered smoothly and twisted away, and made me think of a serpent more than a rodent. And just as Thomas reached me I could swear I saw a flash of white like glittering scales.

My gaze returned to those gathered as if in tableau. The merchant and the Arab appeared withdrawn; the fleet-fingered one still grinned; and the monk's thumbs worked as though he turned a rosary. Thomas touched my elbow and I looked to him with a shaky breath.

"I don't know if we will all make it," I said. My eyes returned to where the white viper had disappeared. "This voyage will be hard, indeed. And I don't know for whom it will be hardest."

Thomas' smile spoke quiet comfort. "But more will find The Beloved, and by him their souls kept safe forever," he said. I returned his smile, though somewhat less assured.

There was a bellow from the decks somewhere, and the mate called out to us. "Captain likes to cast off early, so board now if you want and get stowed."

Everyone rose, apparently eager to be on, even if we were not sailing just yet. We followed the mate up the gangplank. The deck was still bustling with activity as crates, casks, and bales were stored, stacked, and lashed down. The mate led us across and down the ladder belowdecks. The noise faded somewhat, and I felt the first turn of my stomach as the ground rolled under me.

It would be the best I would feel for many days after.

We were led to passenger accommodations, which consisted of a roped-off section of hammocks. Chests were bolted to the deck underneath, one per hammock. I glanced up, noticing a bit of clear stone that let light into the interior. But it was still far darker than outside. From the depths there was motion, and a long man with blond hair unfolded himself somehow from a hammock near the back. He approached at a crouch in the cramped quarters. While he did not smile, there was a stolid cheerfulness that emanated from him. I couldn't help but wonder why a Norseman was so far south and heading further.

"If you have anything you want secured, put it in these and don't lose your key," the mate said as we huddled around. He glanced quickly at the Norseman to include him in the instructions. "If you want it out after that we'll have to break it, and you'll sit on it yerself if you don't trust anyone. If you have a problem, find me. I don't expect you to be in the way topside when we hit rough seas."

"Do you think we will?" the merchant asked apprehensively. The Norseman grinned at that.

The mate glowered. "We will. Too early in spring not to. Unless you want to wait for the next ship, I better hear nothing else about it." The merchant quavered but held his peace. "Meals will be told to you. Don't expect a lot—we're a trading vessel mostly." Again he glowered at the merchant before continuing. "We've got a full crew, but we still might need some help from those as can offer it. For your passage, I expect you to give it. Any questions?" When there were none, he continued: "I'm Mister Fields—that'll do for it, anyway. Your Captain is Gavril; he should be addressing you once we're out to sea." He moved past us, then turned quickly back. "Oh, and we should have more joining us soon, so don't spread out." He glanced over the hammocks as though counting to make sure there would be enough. I wasn't sure how to interpret the thin set to his mouth, as though it would be short.

We stood awkwardly in the dark a moment. It was the Norseman who spoke first, his accent thick. "Well, this will be a fine voyage," he said, grinning broadly at all of us. "I am called Agnarr."

"Khalid," said the other Arab.

The merchant swallowed, shifting his foot as the ship rolled. "Langford," he said. "Much of what's here is my lord's, so he wished me to go with it."

Several pairs of eyes glittered at him. Agnarr laughed, clapping a meaty hand on Langford's shoulder. "Keeping it safe?" he asked.

Langford laughed nervously. "No, of course not. I'm no warrior. But it is not yet sold, you see." He swallowed again.

I gave our names, including Mahmoud.

"Oh dear," said the one I thought to be a monk. "I had taken the name Thomas also. Well, call me Robert, then, after my second name."

My gaze lingered on him, still wondering, until the final one spoke. "I was called Robert once," he said, though the spark in his eyes told me he was lying. "Too many were looking for it, so now I go by Adloth. My stage name." His smile widened, showing his teeth as another coin appeared and disappeared from his hand.

"Oh, how lovely!" Robert said, clapping with delight. "I won't mind some entertainment on this voyage."

"Is that how you pay your way?" Agnarr asked. He seemed less enthusiastic.

Adloth shrugged. "I do what I can."

I swallowed as the ship pitched especially hard, and Thomas and I both stumbled a step. "I might go back up the stairs," I said quietly.

"It's called a ladder, aboard a ship," Agnarr said, but he gestured that I could lead the way. I smiled thinly, trying not to hurry to them. Thomas was below me to steady me, and the rest of the passengers were not far behind. As I came up, the bustle seemed a little less, and I breathed the open air gratefully. It seemed to help. I moved away to let everyone else come up.

"You will get used to it," Agnarr comforted me as he came up. I turned to thank him, but froze. I was accustomed to looking upward at Thomas, though he was only a little taller than I. But Agnarr was enormous in height and in the breadth of his shoulders. Hunched as he had been below I couldn't tell. Now I almost couldn't understand it—I had never seen one like him. None of the Norsemen who had passed through the convent were as tall, that I could remember.

As he peered down at me he grinned again as if he understood. "You'll get used to that as well," he rumbled. "I'm unusual even among my people. From my family come the legends of the frost giants." He bellowed a laugh, and though it frightened me some then, it was a laugh I would grow to long for as the voyage continued.

Right then, I only stuttered something nervously, and turned my gaze to the ocean. The horizon stretched endlessly away and moved slowly up and down. "It'll be worse once we've cast off," a liquid voice crooned. I turned quickly to see Adloth's malicious grin. Thomas was distracted by Agnarr, probably learning more about ships. "The ropes holding us to the dock steady us a little bit." His gaze went outward, his grin became a smirk. "Nothing to hold onto out there, though."

I felt the Flame waver, then steady. "There are other anchors," I said. "And I've adapted to much since we've begun our travels."

He raised a brow. "Indeed? And from where cometh you?"

"Away north," I said simply. "A town called Holden."

"Out to see the wide world, are you? Not as simple as home life, I imagine."

It was my turn to smirk. "My life has not been simple for a few years now," I said. I eyed him as he held his silence. "How many voyages have you been on?"

His eyes flashed just briefly, but he only smiled and turned away. I watched him go, then looked at Thomas. "Does that mean 'none'?" I murmured. Thomas only shook his head chidingly. I lifted a shoulder: Adloth had started it.

I stayed on deck as darkness fell, the stars brilliant overhead. A few sailors stood guard, torches lit on six points of the railing. I had heard few stories of the ocean, but all failed to mention the stink of the wharf. Anything slightly liquid in town seemed to drain into its waters, and only rarely washed out to sea. Dead fish floated and bumped against the docks until scavenging birds finally cleaned them up, though there were also a few dead birds and no one to clean up those. And the water itself brewed brackish and brine together. It made prayer difficult, but not as difficult as being cramped below, so I stayed topside.

At some point, the Captain emerged from his cabin and walked a circuit around the deck. Though he touched nothing, I could tell he inspected all. When he came near he seemed to inspect me as well. He had a head full of hair, midnight-black, tied in the back and two corners of his beard in braids. His eyes were sharp, piercing blue, and he didn't smile.

"You are Rae-Anna," he said.

I smiled tentatively. "As the only woman passenger, I suppose I must be."

"Another will join us tomorrow. Your husband is Thomas?"

"Yes."

"Fear nothing from the crew," he said. I smiled my thanks. "But I cannot guarantee the ocean."

"So everyone keeps telling me."

His eyes lifted to the dark horizon, seemed to relax as they held there. "You travel with the Moor?" he asked as his eyes returned to mine.

I hesitated. "Mahmoud, yes. Is that all right?"

"Have you known him long?"

"Not especially. I suppose I don't fear him, if that's what you're approaching."

He finally smiled, even if it was barely a flash. "Nor should you. I ask because he has made this passage two dozen times at least, always alone or with one other Moor, and always with four or five mules of goods." He paused while I stared. "I wondered if you knew why he was traveling so light. And...forgive me—with you."

It took me a moment to gather myself. Obviously I had an idea why Thomas and I may have been special in his sight, but I could not think we alone warranted losing such a chance on trade. Surely with so few packs he would be at a loss. "I have not known him long enough to answer that with surety," I said slowly. "But my husband and I have tended to bring change wherever we go."

In the Captain's generally-expressionless face, the flattening of his eyebrows amounted to consternation. "Good change or bad?"

I couldn't help but look away. "Good. In the end."

He looked about to say more when a clattering of wheels on the wharf called his attention. He hurried away without excuse as a carriage stopped near the foot of the gangplank. I walked closer to watch as the footman hopped down and hurried to the door. The first out was a portly man in silks and what I ungenerously thought of as a ridiculous hat. His mustache and beard were well-trimmed, making Langford's seem unkempt. He wiped his brow quickly with a handkerchief as he turned back to the door and extended a hand. A slender, gloved hand appeared, followed by a lady as she ducked through to give the long feather on her hat clearance. She straightened on the steps, every inch the elegance that even Lady Pendrel didn't possess. Behind her came two children, both under ten years old, a little prince and princess if I had to guess. That they were hers was obvious, even in the near-dark. And twins, if I had to guess, as their heads turned almost synchronously to take in the wharf and ship.

"My lord, I was not expecting you tonight," Captain Gavril called as he strode down the plank.

The lady stepped down before the lord turned. "You know Ms. Charlotte, Gav," he said with a slight wheeze to his deep voice. "When she's ready, she's ready."

She rapped the lord lightly on the chest with her fan. "That is not true, daddy, and you know it." She turned to the Captain. "He loves to embellish. The truth is I wanted a night aboard to get used to it. As I always do," she added with a pointed look at her father. He rolled his eyes and shrugged expressively.

"I hope we don't inconvenience you, Gav," he said. He glanced up just then and caught sight of me. He hesitated before giving me a cursory grin to acknowledge me. I only nodded gravely. It felt appropriate somehow.

Gavril glanced back and caught sight of me as well. "As it happens, the rest are already on board," he said as he turned back. He looked across them. "Is this...forgive me, I was expecting more."

"Oh, their nannies came down ill yesterday. We'll be attending them," Charlotte said. I wondered for a moment, but then noticed both children standing very still and stoic. They observed the conversation with a gravity well beyond their years.

"Of course. Then, welcome aboard your ship, Master Kingsley." Gavril bowed deeply, extending his hand up the gangplank.

"Thank you, Gav," Kinglsey said, making his way up steadier than I would have guessed of a man his age and proportions. Perhaps if he was in some way a shipbuilder, he had more experience than any except the captain himself. Charlotte and her children followed behind, and the footman with two sailors carrying a chest.

I moved aside to where I thought I would be out of the way until they passed. Charlotte caught my eye and stepped over with a broad smile. Her blond hair shimmered almost orange in the firelight of the torches, the shadows making odd planes on her face. She looked at me as one she knew would never otherwise meet her in her station, was no threat, and therefore it was all right to be kind. "Just us two women, I'm told," she said in low tones. "We'll have to spend much time together to while away the crossing."

I curtsied. "Of course, milady. I hope I do not bore you."

Her sparkling eyes took in my face, and I nearly looked away. "Oh, I think I will find you most fascinating," she murmured. She touched my cheek with a finger before walking away. Just before she made it to the ladder she took her hat off and threw it unceremoniously over the side. I glanced over as it sank, the white feather slipping below the waves with barely a ripple.

If she did it for luck, it was for the wrong kind. I felt it then, and shuddered.

Chapter 2

I had never heard as much snoring in my life as I did that first night, and I slept terribly. I wanted to roll over, but could not in the hammock. The backs of my knees would ache and I would have to bend one knee a few times, then the other. Thomas, after so long of being intimate, was a safe distance away again. This journey, though, we handled it better. At least, I handled it better.

Of course, the sea sickness helped.

I managed to doze off and on, and it was from such a doze I was awoken by the cries of seagulls and sailors as the ship prepared to set sail. At a whistle and bellow, three quarters of the lower deck emptied. The two children only barely kept from underfoot as they too surged to the deck to watch the work. I felt unwell and tired, so I remained right where I was.

Thomas paused to glance at me, and in the dimness I could tell he knew. He gave me a pitying grin. "The sailors might know a remedy," he offered.

I swallowed and forced a smile in return. "Agnarr said it will get better." I managed, barely and without grace, to dismount from the hammock. I slipped my feet into the light leathers Mahmoud had recommended for the trip and made my way forward. Thomas gripped my hand, lifting it briefly to kiss it before we made our way topside.

In the morning sunlight, the dawn just barely over the water and with a light mist, I marveled at how quickly and surely the crew moved. Mister Fields was pacing the deck, eyes everywhere as he shouted. Though I was no expert, it always felt as though the crew was already doing whatever command he shouted. They seemed to expect it, though. I turned as I surveyed it all, and spotted Master Kingsley near the helm with Captain Gavril. Charlotte stood not too far to one side, both children clutched to her legs to prevent them interfering. The boy struggled occasionally; the girl stood silent. She sometimes glared at her sibling. Though they were twins, I could tell she was taking on the role of elder sister.

"Incredible," Robert murmured beside me. I turned back quickly. His eyes were alight as he watched the sailors scrambling aloft to unfurl sails.

As the front ones bloomed in the breeze, the ropes tying us to the wharf were tossed aboard. I could barely feel a wind just then, yet the canvases floated tight. More shouts from Mister Fields; sailors loosed some ropes while others pulled, and I saw the sails turn and grow tauter. The bow pulled away from shore.

While the bobbing of the deck did not worsen, it felt somehow looser and I swallowed again. Probably just my own mind, now that nothing held us to solid ground. I could not keep my eyes on that beautiful misty dawn, though, so I fastened them to the deck.

"I'm glad I'm not the only one experiencing this for the first time," I said aside to Robert. He glanced at me and I smiled. "Do you mind:

where are you coming from? I feel perhaps conversation will take my mind off the movement."

His smile was guarded, though. "Difficult to say," he said. "Where I'm from, that is. I could tell you that I was born in Chantereaux, though that might mean nothing to you?" I shook my head. His grin eased a little. "I thought not. After that, though..." He shrugged. "Many have been my travels, and varied have been my roads. Wherever the Fire takes me, I suppose."

I felt Thomas turn as he attended our conversation. "Truly?" I asked. "May I ask how long? I only say so because Thomas and I have started down much the same path, though far more recently."

"Have you? Both?" I couldn't tell from his tone if he was shocked, scandalized, or merely surprised. Mister Fields was still shouting. Another mast full of sails had unfurled by now, and we were picking up some speed toward the harbor mouth.

"Yes," Thomas answered for me. He seemed to interpret it as merely surprise. "Not wed at first, though we were chaperoned." He grinned at me. I had to laugh; he was not lying. "Though we made it official after our first stop."

Robert looked out to sea, chewing his lip. "I had never met another," he said finally. "Not who would claim it so boldly, anyway."

"How were you called?" Thomas asked.

He glanced sharply at us. "Called?"

"Sure. I meant, how did the Fire come to you, how did he let you know it was him..." Thomas trailed off, glancing at me as Robert became even more bewildered.

"I never heard of it that way," Robert said. "I was not called, but sent. The monks at Chantereaux questioned me at some length about what the Fire had been doing in my life. It was they who determined I was to be sent, and I obeyed."

"I thought you said you went where the Fire took you?" I asked.

"The Fire as interpreted by the clergy, though." He looked nearly scandalized again. "You mean you interpret it yourself?" He glanced us both up and down, especially Thomas, and did not seem to approve of what he saw.

"Hmm. Well." I said as I considered. I glanced at Thomas and squinted. "I'm not sure how much interpretation we've done. He's usually been fairly clear, or it became clear after we acted."

Thomas nodded agreement. "Also mine has been a Seed. But I grew up a farmer, so I understand that better."

Robert took a step back. "I...see," he said, though I could tell he didn't. "Forgive me if I...well, I shall wait to see. You can imagine why I mistrust such statements, especially from those so young?"

I smiled, remembering St. Timautheo's youth. "Perhaps if we be *an example of the believers, in word, in conversation, in charity, in spirit, in faith, in purity,*" I offered.

"Though you admit traveling together without being wed?"

"Are you wed to Mistress Charlotte?" I asked with a glance to where she stood with her children.

He did not look back. "I do not confess attraction or even admiration of her," he said.

"These remained well separated before they wed," Mahmoud said, behind us suddenly. I startled, but turned with a smile. He did not yet return it as he stared at Robert. "I know the word of a Moor means little," he continued. Robert's open mouth shut as though Mahmoud had taken the words out of it. "But what Rae-Anna has taught me of your god is final judgement of the heart is up to him. If you have her Fire, perhaps you can ask it the truth of them."

Mahmoud left Robert a little redder in the face. After an awkward moment Robert departed as well, only muttering: "we'll see." I grimaced at Thomas. We had not been so thoroughly doubted since the convent. I was surprised, though perhaps I should not have been. We still were not orthodox.

Adloth, it soon turned out, was right: the rocking became much more pronounced once we reached open seas. I thought casting off was enough, not realizing how calm the bay kept the waters. But very soon we were plunging ahead as though mounted on a hundred horses. The scurry on the deck faded away, though a few of the youngest were kept busy. The twins were finally set loose and ran from bow to stern and side to side looking out over every quarter of the ocean. It was then I learned their names were Ginnie and Jonnie, at least as they were called by Charlotte. Master Kingsley merely lit a pipe and puffed, occasionally glaring angrily at them if he saw a sailor nearly stumble over them.

When the port lay nearly gone from the horizon, the Captain finally descended. Mister Fields joined him, motioning all the passengers to assemble. I leaned into Thomas to support myself. He seemed to stand a little solider on the deck than I could, still.

"Welcome aboard, more officially," Gavril began, casting his eye graciously across us all. "I am in the habit of speaking to all of my passengers once we're well underway. This time is of greater note, as Master Kingsley, here, has furnished us this ship. It is his most recent build, and he asked to sail its maiden voyage. I was most happy to oblige." He bowed to Kingsley, and Charlotte clapped. Robert, awkwardly, joined her near the end.

Gavril straightened. "I know Mister Fields has given some instructions, but I wish to re-affirm them: as part of a reduced fare, you may be called upon to assist if we need more hands. The, uh, women will also do whatever they are capable of," he added with a cautious glance at Charlotte.

She beamed. "You know very well I've been on too many seas to wait to be asked," she said.

"Yes, well," Gavril continued, and I could tell he tried not to look at me. "Just re-affirming. As long as no one is underfoot. Our crew was hand-picked by myself and Master Kingsley, and will get us safe to our port. Any questions for now?" When there were none, he nodded. "Very well. If any should arise, see Mister Fields first. Otherwise, enjoy your trip."

"Thank you, Captain," Adloth said.

His voice grated on me, and I turned my head toward Thomas. Gavril merely smiled and turned for his cabin, along with Master Kingsley. While the rest of the passengers dispersed, I looked up at Thomas. I could see in his eyes some of what I felt. "There's something wrong about him," I murmured. He nodded, then frowned over my head.

I turned back and saw Gavril halted before his cabin, his posture stiff as his eyes searched the horizon. The winds were shifting and I heard a strange, watery groan. I could not tell where it came from. I followed Gavril's eyes, saw on the formerly-clear horizon a great bank of clouds like mountains, dark as pitch except when lit from underneath by flashes of purple and blue.

Gavril was dashing back to the helm. Mister Fields was shouting orders again as the sails shifted and the helmsman turned the ship westward.

"Why don't we just go back?" I murmured to Thomas.

"Because we haven't paid him to take us out and then back," Thomas replied. I detected the faintest hint in his voice of the worry I felt. He smiled down at me. "I'm sure he knows what he's doing," he said.

But my Fire would not be silenced so easily. I pushed away from

Thomas to propel myself toward the helm. "Captain," I called out. I hesitated, worried I was being too free with the Holy Words. *I am not The Little Apostle. And yet, I know what I felt on the shore.*

Or do I?

"I think we may suffer great loss if we keep on," I called out to him.

Thomas was behind me, touching my elbow. "I thought you said we would make it, though?" he murmured.

I looked down, shaking my head. "It might not have meant on our first attempt," I replied quietly.

"I thank you, Miss," Gavril called back. "But I always outrun at least one storm by setting out so early."

I turned back, seeing the great thunderheads spreading wide and approaching fast. "It might not be this one, though," I said.

I don't know if he never heard me, or just continued to ignore me. I could not blame him: I was no Captain.

But halfway through our first meal, I dropped my goblet as the ship pitched suddenly sideways. Everything unsecured ended up on the side of the cabin, and before the ship was righted, a terrific crash of thunder pounded the timbers. Gavril was out the door before the echo faded, and water poured like a waterfall upon the deck outside.

The men were not too far behind, Agnarr leading the way. Charlotte was shouting something in my ear, but for the storm outside I couldn't hear her. When she pushed the twins toward me, I finally understood and made my way below-decks with them, hand-hold by hand-hold.

"I want to see it!" Jonnie complained. Ginnie rolled her eyes. I tried not to feel sick as the ship pitched end to end. Of course our hammocks were near the stern. At least from my vantage point, it felt like midships bucked a little less.

"They want us to be safe," I admonished. Difficult to do when you're nearly shouting.

Jonnie huffed and lay in his hammock. Ginnie gazed at me for a time. "You look terrible," she said, though she did not seem mean-spirited in it.

I smiled. "I feel terrible."

"First voyage?"

I nodded. "Are they all like this?"

She shrugged. "Only in the wrong weather. Summer sailing is the best." She eyed me again. "Maybe you should have waited."

I shrugged. "If I'm told to go, I have to go." I looked at Jonnie, who appeared nearly asleep. "Does that help? Laying down?" I asked Ginnie.

She screwed up her face. "Not for me. You could try, though."

I sat on the hammock, tried uselessly to grip the side to steady myself. After nearly pitching over backward, regaining my seat only by flailing my legs like an upturned beetle, I twisted swiftly to lay down. It swayed side-to-side as well as up and down, and I tipped my head over the side just in time to throw up.

When I finished I wiped my mouth, then climbed back out with a groan. "No, it doesn't work," I muttered. Ginnie only gazed at me. "You've seen this before, I guess." I was, I admit, a little ashamed. But she only nodded solemnly, pointing ahead to where a mop and bucket were secured to a beam.

I fetched them, went topside only long enough to catch some water from the spray drenching the deck. Thomas spotted me in the middle of holding on to some line or other and threw me a concerned look. I could only shrug indifference and work my way back to the ladder below.

How I managed to carry the bucket down without spilling all of it, only The Beloved knows. But under Ginnie's guidance I was able to clean up my mess. Jonnie cracked an eye long enough to see what we were doing and smirked.

Eventually, the rest of the passengers and some of the crew returned belowdecks. "It hasn't eased by much," Adloth said, wiping a hand down his face. "But it has steadied."

"How are you feeling?" Thomas asked, his voice as low as he could make it. He frowned, then sniffed. "Is that…?"

I set my mouth and nodded. "I'm afraid so. I'm okay now—at least, I don't have anything left to get rid of." I watched him as he settled into his hammock. "What do they have you doing?"

He barked a laugh. "Staying out of the way, mostly. Sometimes I have to help pull something tight. I understand about as much of it as I understood chess." I grinned despite my sickness, remembering our attempts at Fosse to teach him. He peered at me to see if I ridiculed him; I did not. "Mister Fields must be a good sailor, though," he continued. "At least he can make me feel like I'm a true sailor."

"He would make a good Norseman," Agnarr rumbled from his berth. "Fields knows the seas, despite his name. And Njordr knows him."

"Who?" I asked.

Agnarr smiled. "God of the sea. He will keep us safe, him and Fields together."

I sensed more than saw Robert cocking an eye at me as though seeing how I would respond. *"They that go down to the sea in ships, that do business in great waters, these see the works of Our Father, and his wonders in the deep,"* I replied.

"That does not comfort me," Langford said wearily. "If these are his works, does he mean to destroy us?"

I smiled. *"Then they cry unto Our Father in their trouble, and he bringeth them out of their distresses. He maketh the storm a calm, so that the waves thereof are still. Then are they glad because they be quiet; so he bringeth them unto their desired haven."*

Langford grunted at this, and even Robert seemed mollified. But that was harder to tell in the dark. "Well I hope he hurries up with it," Langford muttered as the stern mounted the heights and dropped again to the depths.

I couldn't help but agree. I glanced across to where I saw Mahmoud and Khalid conversing. Mahmoud faced away, and his gestures were tight and intense. They kept their voices low, and I could not hear them above the storm. But whatever it was, Khalid seemed unconvinced. Disgusted, at times, on some particular point. I frowned, wishing I could hear them.

"I was assured by the Brothers that I would meet no demise by this voyage," Robert said suddenly. And quite firmly. "I think that is enough to convince me, anyway, to lose no sleep over this weather."

I glanced at him. I had felt the Fire assure me similarly, and yet... "Demise does not mean hurt, does it?" I asked. I wasn't sure why I debated him, but it irked me anyway.

"What does hurt matter, as long as I still live?"

"The rest of us could be dead," Langford replied. "Good to see you and your brothers care about that."

Agnarr broke in: "My Vala also told me I would find success here. And I am less afraid of the sea than others."

"And I don't think the children are benefitted by dark suppositions, Mister Langford," Charlotte added as quietly as the storm allowed.

I glanced at the twins. Jonnie was rapt with attention; only Ginnie seemed worried, but that only barely so. Perhaps she had supreme faith in her grandfather the builder. So perhaps Charlotte said it for her own good, despite her air of experience.

Langford murmured his apologies and we went silent as the waves boomed and crashed, and the rigging creaked. I felt a brief pinch of hunger that made it halfway up my throat before dying. I laid down again, closed my eyes—easier to do now I had nothing to give—and prayed.

I awoke in the darkness. The storm sounded no less. I shifted, trying to find a comfortable position to return to sleep. If I could somehow sleep through the entire storm—

But in a far corner, two red dots gleamed steadily. I blinked a few times, and they wavered as they moved across the floor. In a flash of lightning that reflected off the walls I saw the white serpent as it slithered, head held high almost as though it had hind legs to walk on. It moved effortlessly between the swaying hammocks, eyes locked onto mine. I checked a sigh, waiting to see what it would say.

As though sensing my indifference it halted. A pink tongue, not forked, slithered out and waved through the air. It—all I can think is that it grinned, every tooth fang-sharp. It turned, moved to Langford's hammock and slithered over top of him. He twitched as if in a nightmare, snorted once, then calmed as the serpent plopped to the floor again. It went next to Adloth, with the same result. Adloth's hand twitched as though to grasp something, but waved harmlessly through empty air. He grimaced, a sharp rictus as though wounded deeply and something nearly like a cry came out.

I lifted my head to watch as the serpent continued on, this time pausing next to Ginnie's hammock. It poised a moment, those glowing eyes regarding me malevolently.

"No," I commanded.

The tongue slithered out again, and—unheeding—it slithered over her small body. Her hand, this time, shot out and grasped the serpent.

But as soon as her fingers closed around it she screamed, bolting upright far faster than I could manage. She clasped her wrist, staring at her hand as she continued to shriek. Everyone was up in an instant, including most of the sailors, worn as they would be. We rushed over; I couldn't understand, now she was awake, why she still cried.

Charlotte was beside her, comforting her as she sobbed. I fought the rolling deck to come alongside. When I made it, I nearly wished I hadn't.

Her hand was burned, blistered in some places. And where the burns pulled away flesh, silvery scales like a serpent shone through.

Chapter 3

The ship's surgeon was able to soothe the burns, though no one knew what to do about the scales. They did not seem part of her, and her skin appeared and felt like any other skin but for that pattern and color. I worried for a time that, as I had commanded the serpent not to touch her dreams, it had somehow touched her reality instead. But that made little sense either.

I explained little: no one on the ship, other than Thomas and perhaps Mahmoud, would know what to do with the information anyway. And I could see the serpent nowhere, once the chaos had settled down. It had slid its tail into the shadow and disappeared.

The sky grayed the next morning, and the rain continued to fall in sheets as the waves mounted endlessly to the horizon. I managed to bring myself topside for some air. I clung to the railing in prayer and contemplation.

"Well, it is no squall," Captain Gavril said. I twisted to look at him, wretched creature that I was, as he stood firmly in place. His eyes were on the waves, blinking only occasionally in the driving rain.

His gaze finally met mine. "What danger do you speak of?"

I futilely wiped seawater from my face. "I know we will encounter some harm," I said. "But not death."

"And little Ginnie?"

Despite the storm I heard something in his voice, or perhaps saw it in his eyes. Maybe the Fire gave it to me. "I cannot say for certain," I replied, studying him. "She is...your niece?"

He was silent, though his lips tightened. He bent a little sideways as water crashed over the railing. His gaze swept around the horizon again, then returned. "Get below, if you can," he said. "It's about to get worse for a time."

I gulped, and obeyed. When another wave hit, I all but fell in through the hatch to the deck below. I lay for a moment, checking for broken bones. When my blood stopped thundering in my ears, I heard a faint whimper from the passenger quarters. I searched the gloom, but saw only Langford there.

That is unjust, to say 'only'. Fear can strike anyone. I made my way back, yearning for the Fire as I climbed once again ungracefully into my hammock. "Are you well, Langford?" I asked.

I heard scuffling, then a short sigh. "I will do all right, I suppose," he said as manfully as he could.

I hummed a moment. "Weathering storms is rarely easy," I said, then paused. "The storms of our dreams can be even harder."

"Do you have nightmares?" he asked. I could tell he was trying to be conversational, but the quiet intensity assured me I was on the right path.

"Oh, many. Thomas and I both have seen things that are hard to shake. Sometimes they even haunt our waking moments. At least then we can rest more easily in The Beloved. But at night..."

He grunted. "Robert was saying much the same thing, earlier," he said. "He said I should see one of your holy men as soon as we reach Algiers."

"The Beloved is with us everywhere," I replied. "We needn't wait until then." The silence stretched. "If you wish to tell me, I could—"

"I don't know if…" He trailed off, and I thought perhaps he only wanted to interrupt. But I let him rest. There was some shouting above, and the ship pitched a little off-center from its normal up-and-down. Boards thumped over our heads and the rush of water intensified. A sheet of it fell through the hatch, splattering on our deck. Thunder boomed.

It quieted again, and Langford spoke up. "You said Thomas, too, has your Fire?"

I smiled. "He does. He would be happy to listen as well."

More thunder, then pouring water. A sailor came down, but continued to the lower deck where the cargo was stored. When he came back he was muttering, though he did not seem too distraught just yet. The thunder still sounded, though quieter, and the rain faded to a rhythm. My eyes fluttered as I rested in the Flame.

"Why do you think we dream?" Langford asked.

I blinked. Somehow I had nearly slept. I shifted my weight up higher in the hammock. "There are some who think every dream is a sending," I replied. "If so, I've no idea what I am supposed to learn or take heed from walking through a home I've never visited, or leaning so far into my step that I fall on my face." I smiled for no one's benefit. "Perhaps much of it is just our imagination. Without hearing what you've dreamed, though…"

"Most of mine are the same as you describe," he said, and I thought I could hear the smile in his voice. He cleared his throat. "Last night, though. Well, it started like one of those. Then, suddenly, I was in Jenois again. The beginning of a lovely summer day, the kind my mama would pack us a lunch and we would climb the hills until home was tucked below us among brilliant green and marble. Papa sometimes would meet us smelling of sunlit grass and new lambs." He broke off, cleared his throat again. "Well, we didn't do all that, but it reminded me of those kinds of days. But I couldn't go. My lord had already set the sale, and I had to go with it. I kept looking at the sky, thinking of the hills, distracted from the products he'd sent me to get. To inspect, that is. They were paid for. I thought they were. But it was a large order, and as I say, I was distracted from it, and somehow I was at my lord's manor with broken crates half empty. The merchants were long gone, and I had squandered his monies. I was cast out. Banished. So I chased them down, the merchants, but couldn't get to them. Finally, I nearly had them in an alley when suddenly the buildings beside me clamped shut over top of me like a giant maw." He finally paused for breath, gasped a few times. "My lord caught up to me, spat on me, and wiped his shoe off on my face. Then I awoke."

"You said you *thought* they were paid for, as though they were not," I said slowly. "But then you had squandered your lord's money."

"I can't remember," he said slowly. "I think they claimed they had only given half the order because that was all they had received. And yet my lord claimed he had sent them all the money. So he knew I had stolen it—" He cut off, and a moment later I heard his feet thump to the deck. "I might see if..." But he trailed off before hurrying topside.

I lay, swaying in the dark, for how long I do not know. Thunder came and went; water cascaded at some times, others it was silent. Voices neared the hatch, then descended. I glanced over, saw Adloth and Robert catch my eye. Their conversation ceased as they moved to their separate hammocks.

"How is it out there?" I asked, fighting a sudden rise in my throat.

I closed my eyes and tried to return into the Fire.

"It still rages," Robert said first. "Of course Gavril cannot know for how long…"

"It has only been a day and a night," Adloth murmured. I cocked an eye on him; it was the least confidence I had yet heard in his voice.

"Storms are always interminable in their midst," I said. When he glanced at me I grinned. "Physical as well as spiritual."

He grunted. "You may have experience with the latter," he said. "But I've more of the former. This one is peculiar."

"How so?"

I could faintly see the whites of his eyes sway in the dark as he shook his head. "I have been at sea in storms before. They do not seem so…endless as this one."

I did not argue, for I could hear the sincerity in his voice. And, truth be told, something in the Fire gave me the same sense. That, and the spiritual experience to which he referred told me this was not a natural storm only. "We all must seek The Beloved," I said. "He uses this to get our attention."

"Did your Fire tell you that?" Robert asked.

I bit back hard against the derision in his voice. "It does, sir, as it did when Thomas and I stood on the wharf."

"Then why are you here?" Adloth asked.

"As Robert suggested, this is not the first storm I have been called into. Our Father sees all of history in a sort of storm, and I am quite certain He calls his followers not to be safe from it, but to rush headlong into it. Only by doing so may we save all afloat."

There was silence a moment, before Adloth spoke up again. "And what say the Brothers about that, Robert?"

"I could not say," he replied instantly. "There are many who stay in their cloister to give shelter from these storms."

I grumbled to myself. Of course he had the right of it—I had said as much to the Sisters at Holden. "But how many use that as an excuse!" I said instead. "Who use such thinking as their own shelter, while countless perish in hopelessness." I shook my head with a sigh. "But they will answer, I suppose. For me, I am here and Thomas is here as we are bid."

I felt Robert's eyes burning into me, but ignored him. Well, if it pricked his conscience, it was supposed to. Finally he got up and went to the hatch, disappearing through the patch of gray daylight. When his foot left the last rung, my heart smote me. If he was a brother—and I had to assume he was in truth—I treated him horrendously. Yet something still nagged, kept my lips thin and my arms crossed in my hammock.

"Langford said you listen to dreams," Adloth murmured.

The Fire flickered, touching the bottom of my heart to warm it. I wiped a tear I hadn't realized had squeezed from my eye. "Yes," I said shortly.

"Can you interpret them?"

"Not I, but Our Father," I said automatically. I turned my head fractionally. "In truth, He has not given me such a gift as yet. But He has given me some wisdom here and there. And a kind ear, I think." That may have been a lie. Or only sometimes true.

"And a closed mouth?"

"As needed."

"I would rather chance it with you than another." He lay silently for a time. He started to speak once, but was silenced by a terrific crack of thunder. I found myself holding my breath, waiting for the sound of a spar to smash upon the deck. Perhaps he waited as well. But the ship pitched on until finally he began again. "My dreams last night began pleasantly enough," he said, as I assumed he would. Pleasantly, until the serpent touched him. "I was once with a traveling troupe, as you may have guessed. I did well enough, but not as well as I would have liked. Until my skill was perceived by another, who made me a most lucrative offer." He paused for another roll of thunder. "Well, I was back with that troupe in my dream, playing one of our last shows together. At court." He paused, and I again saw the whites of his eyes wagging. "Harmouth thought it was our next step up, to a new plateau of performing. Either way. It didn't happen. But in the dream we were playing, and I had mounted Jacob's Ladder as I had done a thousand times before. This time though, a leg collapsed. I saw when I went up they were sound, they always were. But high up, it broke. I teetered, bethought myself that to jump offered survival better than riding it down. But my foot caught in a rung. I clutched at the ladder as though something might catch it, might suddenly make it secure. I swung nearby a tapestry, reached out for it, but it was too late. As I fell I looked suddenly at Harmouth, perceived the small saw in his hand as he smiled at me. As I struck the ground I awoke, and young Ginnie was screaming to match my own in the dream."

I drew a breath as I glanced back toward her hammock. She stayed in the surgeon's quarters, still. "What happened to the troupe after you'd gone?" I asked.

"Harmouth tried to go on, took another billing with some Duke or other. My replacement wasn't ready." I saw his hammock shift as though he shrugged. "Fool that he was," he muttered.

"So you cut the leg off him and made him topple," I pressed. I wished it was bright enough for him to see my gentle smile as I tried to give it. "My point is, you perhaps feel some guilt? Or think of how it might affect you if he did something similar to you. *Therefore all things whatsoever ye would that men should do to you, do ye even so to them.*"

"Fine for you, perhaps," he spat, and his hammock creaked as he rose. "In the real world, fools like that are taken advantage of."

Before I could offer anything else he was gone up the ladder. I remained swaying, thinking. Two men touched by the serpent, two terrible dreams of past sins. But neither showed regret like those of Fosse. And a storm outside that felt bottomless.

I wished Robert would come down again. I wondered if he ran away from a hard command by the Brothers, for all he said he followed the Fire. Perhaps this storm was something akin to Jonah.

But when I heard footsteps again it was Thomas, followed closely by Agnarr. A weight lifted, and I found it strange it seemed tied to Agnarr more than Thomas. Both approached, ducking under and around the empty hammocks.

"The Norseman can have a storm like this," Thomas said, swiping water from his face. He gripped his short tail, squeezing water from his hair.

Agnarr laughed. "It is a good ship, and new," he said. "Its timbers will not break soon."

"I'm not so worried about the ship breaking apart," I said. Thomas' hand was on my arm. I laid my other hand on his. "It's not so bad. But it doesn't seem to be getting better."

"Here," Agnarr said. "I needed it not earlier, but my Vala prophesied I should bring it with."

He pressed something into my palm; it felt like a root. "What is it?" I asked, drawing it closer and sniffing it. It smelled sweet, almost citrusy.

"Chew it," he said. "Not to eat, but distract you. Just a small piece. Worry it."

I nipped off a bit, worked it around. It was spongy, but did not quickly break apart. I felt my stomach ease just a little. "I think it works," I managed. "Is this all you have?"

He laughed his hearty laugh. "You will not need so much. It will get better soon."

But for three long days and nights, it did not. Rain pelted, thunder boomed, waves stretched into an endless dark. The ship was taking on more water, and more of the crew were given to bailing it out again. Langford paced when he could, worried Gavril would order the goods thrown overboard.

For his part, the Captain did not immediately deny it. And Langford nearly wailed, wringing his hands.

Ginnie returned belowdecks, though she and Jonnie both sat pensively on their hammocks. Charlotte stayed with them, now, humming a gentle tune. We'd had dinner, such as it was. Agnarr's root helped me eat without throwing it immediately back up again. I couldn't help glancing at him from time to time, taking comfort in his broad shoulders, easy posture, and his constant smile as though a laugh just waited to be released.

It eased some of the tension in the hammocks, though not by much. The sailors came and went in their shifts, muttering quiet curses if they spoke at all. We knew it was not going well. The journey should have been half as many days, and Charlotte let slip that there would not be enough food for much longer.

And so we remained mostly silent with our own thoughts, or letting them run with what snatches of conversation we heard from the sailors. Perhaps not the soundest of ideas, but it was all we had. Thomas was holding my hand and I could tell he prayed. I squeezed, rubbed my thumb on the back of his hand, and tried to pray, too.

"I'd rather the sailors' curses," Adloth muttered harshly. I stuttered, then gazed at him. "Those seem more useful to me, at least for venting frustration."

"Our Father will get us safely through this," Robert intoned. "Not just me, not just those two. The whole ship will be saved if we hold fast."

Adloth muttered—it sounded like one of the curses he seemed to prefer. But I was staring at Robert. Was he prophesying now, without the blessing of the Brothers? "If you wouldn't mind," Adloth continued in loud tones. "Could you ask your blasted Father why this storm is here to begin with?"

"But Jonah rose up to flee unto Tarshish from the presence of Our Father, and went down to Joppa; and he found a ship going to Tarshish: so he paid the fare thereof, and went down into it, to go with them unto Tarshish from the presence of Our Father. But Our Father sent out a great wind into the sea, and there was a mighty tempest in the sea, so that the ship was like to be broken," I said, still gazing at Robert. I felt Thomas' hand grip mine as though he worried. But wasn't it what the Fire gave me?

"How was the ship saved?" Langford asked in the silence.

"Jonah was cast into the sea," I said.

Bile rose in my throat again, surprising me as I fought it back down. At the same instant a cry rose from topside, of mortal terror and hurried prayers. We all looked to the hatch as the confused shouts continued, until curiosity overcame us all and we rushed for the ladder, leaving the twins behind.

I was near the back, heard the exclamations before I could see. The rain still swept down in sheets, stinging my eyes. The crew stood as statues, all facing the back. Some held lines slack in their hands. Most simply stared.

I fought myself to my feet once through the hatch, and turned. In the darkness, I could see nothing at first but mounting waves. I glanced at Thomas, whose gaze aimed higher. I turned, and looked up.

Great red orbs swirled, perhaps two ship-lengths behind us but above our own ship's crow's nest. Far, far above. In a flash of lightning, white scales glittered like pearls on the body of a serpent twice the thickness of our ship as it coiled above the waves. To ride the water so, it had to have been many times longer than what we could see.

"Lindwurm," Agnarr breathed, for the first time ever his ready laugh gone. "It girdles the world, devours longboats."

Another flash and thunder, and the mouth full of fang-sharp teeth grinned as it leered down at us all. And from the hatch we heard Ginnie cry out, her voice copied in the Lindwurm's exultant call.

Chapter 4

I stumbled below, my mind reeling from more than seasickness—though that was still very much present. I barely registered the others following me. I lurched to my hammock, rolled into it with an ease that belied my lack of experience.

"Rae-Anna, what is it?" I heard Thomas say.

How he knew this was not just a reaction to a gargantuan sea serpent, I can only assume his Seed. But my mind would not put words together just yet. I kept my eyes squeezed shut, letting their conversation go into and through me.

"It is Jörmungandr," Agnarr said. "The World Serpent. I had not expected to see him in my lifetime." He paused, and added quietly: "I wonder if Ragnarök approaches."

"Did your Vala say this would appear?" Thomas asked.

"She said I would see both the passing and the portent of Thor," he replied. "I thought it was the storm, alone. But yet, she was not wrong."

"Will it…" I heard Langford trail off, probably for the sake of the children. Their spirits wavered like candle flames behind lost windows. I felt every spirit aboard as a flame, nearly extinguished as the storm winds howled and that...serpent hovering. Waiting.

"I don't think so," I murmured. I swallowed another heave. "Would it not have done so already?"

"None have seen it and lived," Agnarr said bluntly. Charlotte made a small noise of protest as Jonnie whimpered. He pressed on relentlessly. "It is seen between flashes of lightning; thunder echoes off its scales. Any who have seen it are far off, and the ship it follows is gone."

"That's my point," I said, humming a moment to still my throat. "Too much time has already passed."

Agnarr made a non-committal noise, but did not argue outright. "I know not what holds it back, if that is so."

"Your seer said you would live," Robert replied.

"As did ours," Thomas interjected quietly.

I winced, shook my head. I was no prophet. Despite what had happened on the shore. If that had been a gifting, it was clearly momentary. For when I pronounced Jonah's example, that thing had appeared. And its offspring had been following us...

Was it coming for its offspring? Maybe what had assaulted our sleep was an infant Lindwurm—or what had he called it?—and it was here to retrieve it. The look was too similar.

But what had that to do with Our Father's Kingdom?

"You believe one of our sins brought this to us?" Adloth asked. I could tell he thought of his dream.

Thomas was silent, probably waiting for me to answer. He was gifted as well, though, and if I spoke again I might throw up. Feverishly I prodded his hand with my little finger.

"We all have sins," he said, firmly enough, though I could tell he was reaching to connect it. "If that were the case, how could we know whose, and what would it achieve? Do any of you have sins you wish to confess?"

The silence stretched uncomfortably, and I raised a wavering hand. *I do.* I peeked just enough to grin, then let it fall when I saw a few faces ease. Just—and I hated to use the word *just*—'a sin' would be too broad. Someone had something un-confessed—something they knew, but ran from Our Father and His instruction.

"Does the Lindwurm have babies?" I asked.

"Forgive me, I spoke badly," Agnarr said. "He is called Jörmungandr. The Lindwurm belongs on land. Him I have seen in the night. But no, Jörmungandr has no children."

"How is Jörmungandr satisfied?" Langford asked. "If he is not here to eat us—"

"Could we please talk of something else?" Charlotte cried. "You are terrifying the children."

The men were silent a moment. Agnarr cleared his throat and lowered his voice. "There is no satisfying him, except the body of Thor," he said. "And only Thor will defeat him. For now I trust my Vala that no eternal harm comes from this."

"Why did you ask about babies?" Thomas asked me gently.

I felt their attention before I cracked my eyes. "I saw something ashore, and again a few nights ago. When Ginnie was injured. It looked like—" I struggled with the name Agnarr had given it, and settled for the easier one. "—the Lindwurm, but the size of a serpent." I saw Agnarr smile, but he left me alone. "But I have not seen it since. I wondered if *that* came for it."

"It gave me my nightmare?" Adloth asked quietly.

I nodded slowly. "At least, I saw you shudder when it touched you. It went to her as well." I swallowed and shook my head. "I commanded it to leave her dreams alone. It burned her hand instead."

Langford shifted, settling his feet on the deck. "You saw it ashore. Then saw it on the boat, saw it touch us and send evil upon us. Whether your command went awry or not, it obeyed you. And then this one appears the moment you tell us about your Jonah." He cocked his head and snapped: "Perhaps you are supposed to throw yourself overboard."

I cast a bleary eye on him. "I have not rejected that notion," I replied. Thomas squeezed my hand, and I turned my wrist. "I listen for the prompting of the Sacred Fire, whatever he wills," I said more firmly. "If it is me, then it is me. But I cannot say he demands any of us, just yet."

"At least that," Robert muttered. I glanced at him. His brows lowered against my gaze. "At least you attempt some humility," he clarified. "However late it may be, perhaps we shall still be spared from untethered opinions."

"As you say," Thomas rebutted, "none of us seem very 'tethered' just yet. I don't hear you offering much security either."

"And I admit it," Robert replied hotly. "I will not be so proud to presume upon understanding Our Father's plans or ways—and certainly not to attempt to exert that understanding upon others as though I were so much wiser. 'It is not good that the man should be alone,' and in the morass of one's own thoughts there is little counsel that is good."

"She is not alone, she is with me," Thomas replied. "And if you noticed, you and Agnarr also doubt our harm."

"Harm, yes! But she would have one of us throw ourselves into the raging seas to appease a bloodthirsty god, as this heathen Norseman would!"

"Jörmungandr demands no sacrifice," Agnarr replied, and I felt the ice of the north in his tone.

"You know very well what I mean," Robert retorted. "Our Father already sacrificed The Beloved. No other is required."

"I only answered a question," I murmured, knowing as well as Robert did it was a false excuse. I wiped my eyes. "Forgive me if you must. No one needs to throw themselves off the boat to this thing. But it is here for a reason, and it has nothing to do with swallowing this ship."

There was silence again except the creaking of the rigging. Even the thunder had gone silent for a time. But I thought, in the silence, I heard some otherworldly murmuring. It grew more insistent. I reached for the Flame, and though it stoked higher than normal it was not truly reaching back.

The murmuring grew louder, and I realized it was in my ears not just my mind. I opened my eyes, glanced toward Thomas. His gaze met mine and he frowned. Almost as one, the several of us searched for the source.

Behind us, finally, we spotted Charlotte, whose eyes were fixed on something we could not see. And yet neither was she speaking, though the sound came from near her. Thomas rose first and went back.

"Ginnie?" he called out softly. He sucked in a breath. "Rae-Anna, if you can…"

I squeezed my eyes shut as I rose, swallowing thickly. A distant rumble of thunder followed me between the hammocks, and as I reached Ginnie a sudden bolt of lightning threw shadows across the deck through one of the prisms. I saw Ginnie's mouth moving, but Thomas was pointing at her arm.

The silvery scales had spread, now covering her to her elbow on unbroken skin. When she looked toward me her eyes blinked red, and her words—now pointing directly at me—washed over me with malice.

"Her?" I wondered. The Fire ensconced me, let her words slide around me as it also lifted the nausea. I watched her a moment, trying to decide, or even discern, what to do. "What language is that?"

"I'm not entirely sure," Thomas said, also studying her. "But she said 'bruni'—wasn't that one of the words they said in Holden?"

"Agnarr," I called back. "Can you hear this?"

He moved forward, listened for a time. Her gaze shifted to him with a sort of evil curiosity, still flashing red when she blinked. I could tell it was not actually Ginnie. Somehow that Lindwurm was moving through her.

"Isn't that Norse?" I asked. I grabbed a hammock as the ship rocked.

He shook his head. "Not the tongue of my people. Maybe one of our neighbors."

A flash of red, and she was back looking at me. Then her gaze roved across those gathered. *"Hvar er sythmathur?"* her voice rasped. She grinned, and I could almost see blood dripping from her teeth. *"Senda mér hann!"*

I looked at Agnarr, his face troubled. But when he caught my gaze he shrugged.

"Your time is limited," I said. A flash of red in the dark. I felt the Fire surge. "Your time is limited," I repeated firmly. "You will harm no one on this ship."

She smiled her bloody grin and lay back. When her eyes closed, the voices stopped and Charlotte awoke from her stupor. She looked down at Ginnie, gasped at her glistening forearm.

"Is it spreading?" she cried. She gripped Ginnie's wrist to look closer at the scales. "What is it?"

I shook my head, my mind reeling with our lessons from the past. "The more these forces enter our world, the more of them we can see," I said. "The more they can interact with us directly."

"But why her?" She massaged the arm; I worried how it might react, but nothing happened.

"They take advantage," Thomas said. "If we allow an opening—well, it can't always take us over without our consent, but they can act to make that consent easier to give."

"I can assure you little Ginnie did not give such a thing an opening," Charlotte replied hotly.

"Not knowingly, of course," I said. "But it might have been a messenger, disguised somehow. And not necessarily one physically seen."

"Didn't you say the serpent touched her in her sleep?" Langford asked. "After you supposedly rebuked it?"

Charlotte's eyes bored into me. "You commanded it? Did you tell it to do this to her?"

"Of course not!" I said. My head swung as another wave of nausea struck me, and my knees buckled. Thomas grabbed me, taking me back toward my hammock.

"It was you!" Langford said. "Every time you deny your involvement with this thing you nearly faint!"

"You have no idea what assaults her in these battles," I heard Thomas reply. All I knew was a sense of reeling, and general precipitation toward lying in that swaying hammock. It felt like the boat rocked on a pin, and I think I threw up again. The argument raged over and around me, and I even heard Agnarr's voice in my defense. That might have hinged more on my being a woman, in his eyes, but the effect was the same. Few wanted to argue outright with one of his size.

The spinning slowed, then stopped in silence. By now, the storm had raged so long I considered it silence, anyway. I was panting, though that was slowing as well. "Where is Adloth?" I asked. I don't know why.

Thomas laid a hand on my arm. I felt it shift a few times. "He's not here. Did he go topside again?"

My nausea drained as from out of an upturned bottle, and I sat up. I moved to the ladder, and though Thomas kept a hand on my elbow, I soon outpaced him. Feet pounded as we all went up again.

It was still dark, rain in sheets, and no lightning to let us see much. Gavril had torches lining the ship, though they were battered by the wind and their light went almost nowhere. Waves and black clouds boiled. Gleaming behind us, before I even turned, was the Lindwurm still coiling and writhing through the ocean in our wake. I gazed up at it. How I kept my feet, I don't know.

"What is it? What goes on there?" Gavril called out.

I looked at him, behind the helm. "Did Adloth come up here?" I called.

He pointed, quickly and wordlessly. Just ahead of midships he stood at the railing between two of the torches.

"Adloth!" I called. "What are you doing?"

His hands gripped the railing, and he cocked his head a little our way as he kept his gaze on the roiling seas. "You heard her," he said. "He wants me." He turned to stare at me, his face pale but determined. "It is me. I have to answer. Ask your Father to save me, if He can."

Before anyone could move he vaulted over the railing, and before I could gasp we heard the splash as he struck the water.

"Man overboard!" Thomas shouted. "Get a rope!"

I turned in place to look at the serpent. Its red eyes bored hungrily into me before his terrible gaze snapped to the water. "Thomas, wait!" I shouted, just as the great head of the beast darted faster than a kingfisher into the sea. I gripped my mouth to keep back a scream. The coils writhed, then suddenly the head reared back from beside the ship. In the torchlight the water cascaded from its mouth the color of blood. Its lips curled into a smile as its eyes found me again, and I saw its throat shiver as it swallowed. Its head wagged as it returned to its place at our stern.

We stood in shock for a few moments. Another flash of lightning lit the sea and the serpent. The blue-white light faded from the sky. I frowned as some of it stayed—the orange light tinged.

"*Madre de Dios!*" one of the sailors cried.

"Rae-Anna," Thomas gasped. I whirled.

One of the torches burned with blue fire, and in the midst of it was Adloth's disembodied head, his face writhing in silent agony.

Chapter 5

THOMAS

When she saw the face of Adloth in the torch, Rae-Anna had doubled over again and I hurried her belowdecks. She lay nearly senseless, but I thought she slept and so I came back topside again to contemplate Jörmungandr and Adloth.

"Is she right?" one of the sailors asked me, terror in his eyes as he stared at the serpent. "Is it because of someone onboard?"

"I don't know," I murmured. I glanced sideways at the torch, taking in Adloth's torment. If it was here because of someone's sin, it clearly was not the magician's.

I tried to keep the sarcasm out of my thoughts, but I struggled. For most of our journeys so far—minus one or two arguments—I trusted Rae-Anna more than myself. At least in this type of thing. I couldn't help but recall Mahmoud's questions in Fosse, when he confronted my faulty logic. Even then I had trusted her explicitly, even if I couldn't toss aside my own fears because of that trust.

This time, I knew something was wrong. Beyond her sickness, she seemed genuinely uncertain. I had rarely seen her uncertain before. She admitted when she didn't know, or was clearly wrong and simply did not realize it—a place more of us find ourselves than we like to admit. But this time, on this voyage and in this storm, it felt from the other side as though the Fire was simply not talking to her.

My Seed, on the other hand, had grown into a forest. So thick, in fact, I had trouble sorting through it to find a solid conclusion either. Verses and scriptures piled on top of one another in such disarray I held my peace around her because I wasn't sure I could bring clarity. At least in part.

I knew that I did not see Jonah anywhere. But I worried that was buried under so many layers of branches, maybe closer to the Seed, and that's why I couldn't see it. That, and I was no prophet.

"Thomas," a familiar voice called. I tore my eyes from Jörmungandr and fastened them onto Mahmoud. I tried to smile, but I'm pretty sure it came out as a grimace. "What is happening?" he asked.

I sighed and shrugged. "I can't say yet," I replied. I tried another grin. "We're a long way from my father's farmlands."

He did not return the grin. But, he rarely did. "We are indeed." He glanced beyond me, and I knew without looking he studied Adloth. "He sold strange wares," he continued, his gaze returning to me. "Khalid did not like him."

"Did he know him before?" I asked. I didn't think a few days was enough to dislike someone.

Mahmoud wagged his head. "They were on the road several days before port. By chance. Adloth's fingers were too light."

"Did he steal from anyone?"

"Never caught." Mahmoud sneered in a way I think I recognized—that it was because Khalid was Arab that no one trusted his word.

"But things were missing?"

Mahmoud sighed, folded his arms. "Khalid trades with a disgraced Moor further east, nearer the Ruus. No one else will trade with him." He shrugged to dismiss what sounded like a long story. "All their papers are in Arabic. He could not prove that either."

I pressed my lips together and shook my head. "I'm sorry, Mahmoud."

He frowned. "Why?"

Finally, a few leaves I could easily read. *"Thou shalt not have in thy bag divers weights, a great and a small. Thou shalt not have in thine house divers measures, a great and a small. For all that do such things, and all that do unrighteously, are an abomination unto Our Father,"* I said. His frown deepened in confusion. "It seems to me if we judge others differently because we weigh their words or worth differently..." I shrugged. "The Littlest Apostle said much similar, though he spoke a little more specifically about those already under The Beloved."

He regarded me strangely for a moment, I could not decide if he found it humorous or compassionate. When his face stilled, he said: "I do not like Khalid."

Now I scowled. "Why not?"

He shrugged. "Because he carries divers weights," he said simply.

I lifted my eyebrows in surprise, but before I could respond, Gavril was shouting orders. Mahmoud and I hurried to respond, along with the other sailors. As near as I could tell, we were trying to let the wind steady us by having some sails lowered and dragging sea anchors. Then, by manipulating the remaining sails, he could turn us into the waves and spare our sides.

"How long can the ship take this?" I shouted to no one in particular. By the grim, set faces of the sailors nearest me, I assumed not forever.

"This isn't so bad," Mister Fields shouted near me. I turned in surprise, nearly losing my grip on a rope as the ship bucked. "At least we're not trying to climb through the waves. And older ships than this have weathered bigger waves."

I felt eased a moment, until I saw one of the sailors roll their eyes when they thought I wasn't looking. I wondered what he knew that either Fields or I did not.

"Alive there!" Fields shouted suddenly, striding around me. A rope had torn loose, and a corner of the sheet snapped in the wind. The rope whipped like a snake as Fields and several other sailors reached for it; one cried out as it struck him in the face. He was on the deck and I saw red mixing with the seawater.

They succeeded in capturing it and running it around a pin. "Take that man below," Fields shouted. "What happened?"

"It's that curse, sir!" another retorted. "Bellerin' along behind us with that wicked grin. Can't blame Deluc if he got sideways for a blink, can ye?"

"I can when he endangers this ship more than that thing is doing," Fields said. "You saw it take the magician. Can any of you move fast enough to get out of its way, if it wants you?" Silence met him as they knew he spoke truth. "Then what difference does it make to look at it or not? If you want to live, do what's in front of you that you can do."

"Aye, sir," they responded. I exchanged a look with Mahmoud.

"I do not know if I have that discipline," he said.

I set myself to face the task in front of me, and I could swear the crystalline light that Jörmungandr put out grew in intensity. I sighed, agreeing with Mahmoud: even behind us, he made his presence seen and felt. And always there was this anticipation of his giant maw suddenly closing around me and yanking me from the deck.

Yet Mister Fields had that point: Jörmungandr had not attacked the deck itself, and when Adloth went over he had struck like lightning. There would be no escape—not if that sea serpent wanted any one of us.

Now the light did intensify, and I glanced sideways to see Jörmungandr's head alongside the ship, his glowing eyes locked on mine. I tried to swallow, but my throat was too dry. He grinned, his mouth full of sharp teeth, before his eyes flicked to Mahmoud, then to one of the other sailors. That one slowly released his hand from a pin where he had just finished securing a rope. He took a step toward the serpent.

"Belay that, sailor!" Mister Fields shouted. "Get back on your line!"

The sailor's throat bobbed and he hesitated. The serpent's tongue slithered out as his mouth gapped and he drew a breath. Another step forward, and suddenly Mister Fields rushed forward. He unsheathed his sword, held it like a spear, and threw it hard towards Jörmungandr's eye.

Without taking his gaze from the sailor, the serpent somehow caught Fields' sword in his teeth, cocked his head aside, and spat. Like a needle flung from a cannon it streaked across the deck and buried to its hilt through the mainmast. Only then did those glowing red orbs shift from the sailor to Fields, and I felt the murderous hate flowing from him.

Lightning flashed out to sea, and thunder shattered the darkness as we all stared mutely. Jörmungandr's smile fell, and in one brief moment as he departed he looked at me. *Can you protect them all, tiny god?* I thought I heard him say as his massive head lifted, and he returned to his place astern.

Another rumble of thunder, and we all stared at each other, then at Fields' sword still quivering in the mainmast. To his credit, he did not even attempt to pull it free. "Back on your lines," he growled. "Not another word about that snake unless it eats the ship."

I swallowed, shifted my grip on the rope. I dived into the canopy of leaves inside, frantically reading each one for some piece of wisdom, some sign from Our Father on how I was supposed to minister to all of these men. But even verses connected to the same stalk held no connection to one another, or contradicted in theme, or were clearly not wisdom. I felt my inside grow dark as the leaves crowded over, and the ones below me seemed to multiply as though the Seed were running absolutely rampant. *Why is this happening?* I felt myself scream inside. Instead of bringing light and life I was about to be smothered. Or was I drowning? I scrambled, fought to come back up and out.

A wave struck the ship, the water dashing me across the face. Mahmoud was there, shouting something. I eased forward, letting the rope slack so we could turn the foresails. When I looked out, the sea mirrored my forest, waves slapping and crashing every which way until I didn't know why it mattered if we faced one way or the other.

I could sense in the tautness of the sailors' faces around me they thought the same. "Reef 'em!" Mister Fields shouted suddenly. "This is getting us nowhere, Captain! Better to just let the sea run us out."

Gavril nodded from the quarterdeck. I tied off my rope. We were not yet required to go aloft to reef sails, so our part was done. But neither did I want to go below. So I watched the sailors swarm the rigging as the helmsman secured the wheel.

"You will not go to Rae-Anna?" Mahmoud asked as we stood out of the way.

I bit my lip, shook my head. "I'm not much use to her right now,"

I said.

Langford found us as well. "Didn't you two say no one would come to any harm?" he asked, flinging a hand toward Adloth's visage.

"I—yes, we did," I said, faltering. I had forgotten. So what did that mean? "Maybe...I guess we better stay on board," I said. Another leaf waved in my face. *"Except these abide in the ship, ye cannot be saved."* Immediately, the leaf shriveled away and fell off. "Think: even when Jörmungandr came alongside he didn't touch any of us—just tried to call that one sailor to him. He didn't even spit Mister Fields' sword back at him, and clearly he could have killed him with it."

Langford folded his arms a moment, then reached out suddenly to grasp a hold as the ship pitched. "It's not a good sign to let us simply be driven along," he said. "We're entering 'last resort' territory."

"You know about these things?" Mahmoud asked.

Langford nodded. "Some," he said.

"Why did the sailor roll his eyes when Fields said older ships have weathered worse?" I asked.

Langford smirked. "Because older ships have settled in. Newer ships have newer wood, to be sure, but they haven't really settled into their caulking. Drive them too hard too soon and they'll break apart like anything else. You're supposed to shake it down, then rest and repair." He jabbed a finger at me. "Then it'll handle a storm like this."

I gazed at him. "You know a lot more than 'some' it seems to me," I said.

He grimaced. "My father was a sailor, wanted me to go into the family business." He shook his head. "I'd had enough before I was sixteen." He looked about to spit, but changed his mind as he gauged the wind.

"Yet here you are," I said, grinning to soften the blow. "Anything from the family business that could help us?"

"Our family doesn't deal in sea serpents," he growled.

I couldn't help but chuckle, despite all. "Fair enough," I said.

"What about you?" he shot back, clearly unappeased. "Where's all this wisdom from *your* Father?"

"I gave some of it," I replied. "Stay on board. I know that much for certain."

He gazed at me a moment. "But you still think it's here for one of us? For something we did?"

I sighed. Maybe I should have gone down to Rae-Anna. And the Forest inside definitely wasn't helping. "Just stay on board," I said. "Sometimes what is confusing now makes sense later."

He glared, flicking his eyes at Mahmoud. "Or we're just biding time to all get eaten once that thing is tired of waiting," he said.

"Our Father is good unto them that wait for him, to the soul that seeketh him," I pressed. Another leaf retracted. I considered it a moment: did I need to repeat everything I saw? Was that how to remove this forest? Had it grown because I neglected to 'prune' it by speaking the words?

I opened my mouth to speak another, but Langford scoffed and strode away. "Ask the Norseman," he shot back. "See if this is what the snake does." He spun quickly to face me. "And if your Father has any say in the matter, anyway!" He disappeared down the hatch, glaring backward at the serpent following us.

I eyed Mahmoud. "What do you think?" I asked.

He wiped the rain from his face as he considered me. "What were you about to say?" he asked.

I set my jaw. Inside, the leaf crinkled as if it withered, and I knew it would be gone if I delayed. I took a breath. *"Our Father is not slack concerning his promise, as some men count slackness; but is longsuffering to us-ward, not willing that any should perish, but that all should come to repentance,*" I said.

"That sounds like the serpent will eventually devour us."

I shrugged. "Maybe he will. Unless our repentance will drive him off before then."

"Why can he not simply save us?" Unlike Langford, Mahmoud asked curiously, though ensconced in his stoicism.

"How, by making us repent?"

He lifted a shoulder. "Can he not do that?"

I smiled. "Does Allah?"

Mahmoud shifted a step as the rain fell in torrents. "Khalid would say it is up to every good Muslim to do that work on earth."

"But you don't."

"I cannot find such a will in the Quran," he said.

I nodded. "Neither can I find it in the Sacred Words," I said. "What I find is an unrelenting love and desire to be with us. For us to choose him, just as I would want Rae-Anna to choose me, not be forced to me." I hesitated. "Marriages are arranged for political or social reasons, I guess. I don't know. Sometimes they work out. But it's not the image of The Beloved and The Church that we find in the Words."

"What does that matter?" Mahmoud asked. "As you said, marriage is for the connection of families. What is love? Pfft." He waved his hands in one of the few expressive gestures I'd ever seen him give. "Love comes, or goes. My family will endure for generations because of my marriage."

"You're married?" I asked in surprise. "And you spend so long away from your wife?"

"She spends it away from me as well," he said, shocked at my own surprise. "Her family trades all across Ifriqiya. Mine comes to Europa. The marriage is not for us to be together, but to prosper each other."

I didn't know what to say. I couldn't imagine it, though some corner of my mind knew most marriages were this way. But I knew as well that when The Little Apostle spoke of the image of The Beloved and the Church, he was not away just so we would prosper, but because the time was not yet ripe. And he longed to be with us, more than I would long to be with Rae-Anna if she was unreachable.

Agnarr approached, then, half an eye on the Norse serpent-god. He wore the ghost of a smile, at least the closest I had seen to one since Jörmungandr appeared. "We are nearly out of the storm," he said.

I frowned. The clouds looked no lighter or darker than before. "How do you know?"

"A Norseman can sometimes tell these things," he said. "The waves…" He motioned like chopping waves. "Their rise and fall, their direction."

"What about him?" I asked, jerking my head toward the stern. "Will he leave when the storm does?"

Agnarr shrugged. "Perhaps Thor will come with the lightning and frighten him away. Unless it is Ragnarök."

"I assume you don't think Our Father can send him away."

"No one sends him away," Agnarr stated with a shake of his head. "As I said, Thor might chase him by force, but he cannot only command him. If Jörmungandr goes, it is because he chooses."

"Our Father has authority over all creation," I said firmly. *"For with authority commandeth he even the unclean spirits, and they do obey him."*

"Jörmungandr is not an unclean spirit," Agnarr replied. "And your Father did not create him. He was born of Loki and Angrbotha."

I frowned, knowing it wasn't true but recognizing his point. There was no mention of Jörmungandr in scripture.

So who—or what—was it really? My reality, and Rae-Anna's, hinged on the Sacred Words. Nothing existed outside its bounds, and we had seen things people would say couldn't exist. Except there had been some tie to scripture. How did this serpent relate?

I realized my mouth was open as though to ask a question, and that Mahmoud and Agnarr waited for it to come out. But they wouldn't know the answer. "I see your point, for now," I said instead. "Excuse me, please."

I went to the hatchway. It was time to return to my wife.

Chapter 6

I vaguely remembered Thomas herding me to the hatchway and down into the hold, and maybe over to my hammock. Beyond that, my mind was blank. I awoke to a tangible darkness, to the ship rocking and pitching. It felt a little different; I couldn't tell why. Charlotte was humming behind me again, soothing the children. I could not even twist my head back to see how Ginnie fared. At least they both rested silently.

The image of Adloth flashed before me, his silent screams in the fire—blue fire, like I had in the convent when the Fire first came to me. Was it coincidence? Or was he bathed in the fires of torment, his unrighteous soul scoured by holiness he could now never attain? All because I opened my mouth.

Be not afraid, but speak.

That mantra had come to me in Aurden, had been a stalwart defense against fear. Now it seemed my boldness caused a man's death. I squeezed my eyes shut in shame, but the blue flame raged higher behind closed eyes and I opened them again.

The humming ceased. I was panting. "Rae-Anna?" Charlotte called. Suddenly she was beside me, her hand on my arm. "What is it? Do I need to get Thomas for you?"

I scrubbed my eyes, gasping to avoid crying. "No, they might still need him. He'll come down when he's ready."

"Very well," she said.

But she didn't leave my side. I focused on her comforting touch, poured all my energy into it and what it signaled. Slowly my breath eased and the Fire crackled as in a hearth. With a final cleansing sigh I asked: "What of you? Can I help you somehow?"

The weight of her hand eased, but did not depart. "I don't suppose—I mean, you speak as if you know things to come..."

I tried not to shut my eyes, to see Adloth again. Just his gaping mouth came to me. "Sometimes," I managed to say.

She gripped me once. "I understand. Of course," she said quickly, though she still whispered as low as she could above the storm. "It's nothing like that. I'm afraid for Ginnie, of course, I don't know what it signals. Does it signal something?"

I shook my head, amazed I didn't send it spinning off again. "I cannot imagine it does," I said. "Like Thomas said, we never see anyone—especially children—compelled beyond their will into evil. But I have seen when evil seems to mark someone, including myself, to make us doubt our position. And so I don't believe the markings will stay once we have figured out how to banish the Lindwurm."

"I thought Agnarr said it was called—"

"I know, I know," I said quickly. "I will probably forever call it the Lindwurm." I shrugged, smiling to myself in the darkness. It was easier to remember, anyway. "But those marks, I'm not sure for whose benefit they are. If they are, as I strongly expect, meant to deceive: deceive who? What do you fear for her, as a result of them?"

"Well, of course I worry it will end up taking her. Or using her for its ends, whatever they are."

"Do you think she'll turn into a serpent?"

"I...I guess I am worried about that. The scales keep spreading as though it will consume her."

I reached over and patted her arm. "Being marked with scales, even head to toe, is far different from being transformed into a serpent, though," I said. "And, forgive me, you seem to leap to that conclusion rather easily. More than others who have not seen the Kingdom of Our Father as manifest as Thomas or I have."

I could see, faintly in a lightning flash, her chewing her lip. "She has always been...odd," she said, her voice so low I struggled to hear it. "Twins they were born, though no two siblings have ever been more different. She, always so studious and mature. Afraid, sometimes, to play. To have fun."

"I had noticed the same, the moment you alighted from the carriage," I agreed. "I assumed she had taken the role of elder. Was she born first?"

"She was. Jonnie seemed content to stay inside." She paused. I assume she was reliving that day. I felt a brief twinge that she had experienced it already, and I could not foretell a date when it might happen for me. But then I felt a different twinge and was content not to be seasick and responsible for a child at the same time. Charlotte continued: "Of course we told her, and yes it fairly went to her head—especially when she wanted her way." She chuckled, then sighed. "But there is more. That, of course, I could accept in a child. Would expect it, even. Power and positioning never really leaves us, even with age. But I suppose...it was one day, I had woken suddenly from a nap. Jonnie was in my lap, also sleeping. And Ginnie was there, staring at him. She didn't realize I was awake. And she wouldn't blink! Even then, the thought of snake ran through my mind—as though she had no lids. The moments dragged by, and as my discomfort became fear, she looked up suddenly and simply informed me that dinner was to be served." Her hand lifted off me to wipe down her face. "It stuck with me for several nights, until finally I explained it away to myself. She could be ever so studious."

"Something changed."

She nodded, the hold dimly lit as Langford descended the ladder. He was grumbling something, sluicing the water off his face as best he could. But he moved to his hammock a little further away and lay down to rest. We both watched him for a time, until Charlotte spoke again. "As we were making ready for this voyage, I had told the children to pack their things. They know, by now, what they need. I had finished overseeing our maid in packing my bag. I came to the stairs, and Ginnie was over Jonnie's shoulder, as though watching what he was putting in. And she was silent. Usually she's guiding him—that's what she likes to call it, acting like she's his mother. But not this time. And I watched for a while, my mind lost in seeing the new ship. And when she looked over at me suddenly, I would swear..." Her hand went to her mouth a moment, and she glanced quickly back to where the twins slept. "Her pupils were slitted, just like a snake, and her eyes lidless. By the time I gasped, they were back to normal, and my little Ginnie was standing there with a question in her eyes. As though she thought I had some detail of packing to point out, and waited for it. Nothing more."

I was frowning, the Fire crackling away inside as though everything were normal. But no hint of help or suggestion came from it. *Anything?* I asked. But no: just hearthfire. I felt it tug a little toward the hatch, but my stomach still roiled and I doubted I could make it up myself. Nor did I want to, if Adloth still burned.

A shadow crossed the hatch as I considered it, and Thomas descended. *Him?* I wondered. He turned—waited, I assume, for his eyes to adjust, then made his way over.

"Rae-Anna," he said. "How are you feeling? Miss Charlotte," he added with a slight bow.

"Better I think," I said. My voice sounded strong to me, at least. Thomas paused, resting his fingertips on my leg. "We were just talking about little Ginnie," I said, "and whether or how her markings relate to the Lindwurm, and all this." I swirled my hands to encompass how vague our understanding was.

He nodded with a hum. "My thoughts were going a similar direction," he said. "I was wondering, though, how Jörmungandr relates to us—to the Sacred Words. What place does it have in our reality?"

"As much as a dragon does, I suppose."

"That's my point," he said. "We have reference to the Dragon in scripture, though—in the Apocalypse. Right? So what about a sea serpent?"

"*Canst thou draw out leviathan with an hook? Or his tongue with a cord which thou lettest down? Canst thou put an hook into his nose? Or bore his jaw through with a thorn?*" I quoted. "From the Patient Sufferer."

Thomas' eyes widened. "When Our Father finally confronted him for his pride," he said. "That's...very interesting. But is that enough?"

"Enough for what?"

"What is chasing us is still something more specifically from another religion, though. It feels...I don't know. Like it doesn't fit."

I shrugged. "It's what we have though. And it doesn't tell us why it's here, or who it's after."

I felt Charlotte stiffen and her hand departed. "Perhaps it's me," she said quietly. "And that's why Ginnie is the way she is. It began with her as a warning to me that I haven't heeded?"

"Is there a warning you haven't heeded?" I asked. "Something you know you should change, and haven't?"

She did not reply immediately, and another shadow passed over the hatch as a sailor descended. He paused at the bottom much as Thomas had, though it seemed with greater uncertainty. He removed a limp hat that he wrung. "Miss Rae-Anna?" he called out. "And is that...Master Thomas?"

"It is," I responded. "Can we help you?"

He took a step forward, and in silhouette I saw his head snap to Charlotte. "Oh, forgive me mistress Charlotte, I dinnae know you were with them."

"It's all right, Eman," she said. "I was about to return to the twins anyway." She patted my arm as she rose and went astern.

Eman came forward, still wringing his hat. "I had a moment to breathe, y'see. We're lettin' her run anyway. And I saw that poor man Adloth's face." He stopped short with a wary glance at me. "I'm afeared, if I may. I had a thought, minded it was idle fancy at the time, that I should nae come on this journey. My missus, see, is a-bed with the wee one back home. But I thought mayhaps we'd need the money, see, if it came to doctors or such."

"I expect you would," I said. "It is not ignoble to see to your own family's affairs."

"Aye, but if I were meant to stay back, and came anyway. I—" He cut off, wrung his hat once more. "Ah, I confess it miss: I dinnae want to stay back with a colicky one, just to hear him cryin' night and day. Am I a terrible father for it?"

I smiled. "The worst," I said gently. "Tell me, you've been a sailor—how long?"

"Near twenty years, miss."

"Your wife has been with you the whole time?"

"Like a saint, miss. Managed our hearth likely better than I ever woulda."

"First child?"

He laughed, then cut off. "Sorry. Nae, missy, we've got twelve wee bairns."

I laughed too. "Eman, I think your wife is more than capable of taking care of a colicky child while you're away. Just make sure she knows how important she is to you, once you get back."

"Aye," he said, his voice soft. He paused. "You think we'll get back?"

"Just don't throw yourself off the ship before we reach Algiers," I said. "And I cannot speak for the return trip. But I can't see the Lindwurm coming for you because of your twelfth child."

"Ah. Yes, surely miss. Just wanted to be sure. Jonah, you said, and all that. Going where he was nae supposed to."

"If Our Father watches over the fatherless and the widow," Thomas said, "he can watch over the only temporarily fatherless."

Eman smiled, bobbed his head, and departed. He paused at the bottom of the ladder as another sailor descended. They looked awkwardly at each other, then the new arrival looked at us. I smiled as invitingly as I could, wondering how many of them would take advantage of 'letting her run.'

They did not all come exactly on the heels of each other, but neither was there enough space for Thomas and me to discuss much. Every sailor came through, confessing this or that odd sin. Most were—as I said, I don't want to call them 'just' a little sin, for all separates us and hardens us against the holiness Our Father desires. But neither I could say that any one seemed to justify the pursuit of the Lindwurm.

Agnarr descended at some point, but simply went back to his

hammock and lay down. Langford, I felt, shifted a particular way as though he had started to listen. Robert stayed topside, though by the twelfth or thirteenth sailor I wished he might come down and hear some of these as well. Just to lighten the load. Despite the Fire inside, it was wearying after a time.

Thomas, I was a little shocked to hear, handed out Sacred Words to nearly every sailor, sometimes several. And, once, I thought maybe he sounded a little lighter in speech, in his bearing. That I suddenly recognized a weight he had been carrying, but only in the context of its absence. But my fatigue kept me from acknowledging or appreciating it in the moment.

There were a few that stood out. A young sailor whose parents forbade his going off to sea, but in—as he called it—a bittersweet twist of fate they had died of plague and so off he went. An older sailor who went to sea to hide from a series of crimes. He had changed his name and would not succumb to our light pressure to reveal the original. The governor would still like his head on a pike, he said. Another who had sought passage one fateful day, thinking to start a new life, only to become so enamored with sailing he stayed on board. He had broken faith, and the one to whom he'd sworn servitude was likely wrathful that he had not come to fill the role.

In each of those, and a few others, the Fire attended a little heartier. Perhaps that was why they remained with me after the final sailor departed and no more came back. But it never burned bright like it used to when it needed me to pay strict attention.

We sat in silence for a moment, and I closed my eyes. I breathed through the visions of Adloth, which still awaited me in the darkness. *It wasn't my fault, was it? I tried to tell him not to...*

But whoso shall offend one of these little ones which believe in me, it were better for him that a millstone were hanged about his neck, and that he were drowned in the depth of the sea.

My lip trembled, though my heart hardened. *He was not so young. He is still responsible for himself. And I told him to stop!*

The one who eats everything must not treat with contempt the one who does not.

I frowned, my stomach flopping again at the thought of eating. But how did that pertain?

"Just because you know something, or Our Father has revealed something to you, doesn't make you better than another," Thomas murmured. I stiffened, and he went on hurriedly. "Or me either. Any of us. Maturity is not tied to age, or even how long we've known The Beloved, is it? *For who maketh thee to differ from another? And what hast thou that thou didst not receive? Now if thou didst receive it, why dost thou glory, as if thou hadst not received it?* We've known for a while now that our calling and gifting is a great blessing and a great burden. Should we be bitter, or say to someone like Adloth or the others 'come up to where we are' and despise them if they don't?"

I sighed. "No. We've said that before too, haven't we." I shook my head. "Do you think one day we'll actually live in what we say we believe?"

Thomas chuckled, and I felt a warmth spread in me. "Yes, of course," he said. "But it may take some time to bring the light and scrub out all the little corners and cloisters. And then when we feel the work is complete, Our Father will lead us into an entirely different wing and set us to work again." He held my hand, tracing with his fingers on the backside of it.

"Do you think the Lindwurm is here for me? Did I say something wrong, and that's what brought it?"

His silence lengthened as he continued running his fingertip from my knuckle to my wrist and back. "I was surprised when you mentioned Jonah being thrown off the ship," he said. "But neither was I receiving anything about Jonah at all. When we were waiting to board, what I saw and what you first spoke of was Paul's shipwreck. Wasn't it?"

I thought back, trying to remember what I had been given. "I could promise the Fire spoke of Jonah to me in that moment. But I think the last part was me. But he had asked, hadn't he? What was I supposed to answer?"

Thomas' hand left mine as he rubbed his lip. "I guess that's true. And yet Jörmungandr did show up right at that moment..."

Langford was suddenly beside us. "Didn't the little one show up before then, though?"

I startled, gasping a moment. "Um, yes, it did. On shore, even."

He grunted. "Marked this ship early, I'd say. And as we learned tonight, there's no shortage of mistakes made by everyone on board. Maybe with all those confessions you just heard, he'll go away. Just needed to frighten us all. Isn't that how it works with you people? Shout all this doom, gloom, and death until we hang ourselves on your beloved cross anyway?"

I lay in stunned silence a moment. I had hoped he was listening to our words of hope and healing, and softening his heart. It seemed harder than ever, now.

"Is that what you came to do, then?" Thomas asked. Rather then surprise or hurt, I heard compassion in his voice, and I waited to see what he would do.

Langford snorted. "Of course not. I already told this one too much. Doesn't matter anyway."

"How so?"

"None of this does. You all just find your way to live with yourselves, I'll find mine. I *found* mine, I should say. And yes, I began to waver for a moment back there. You almost had me convinced. But listening to this sorry lot and all their guilt? Just trying to make their way through a hard world, and you would have them feel terrible for it, scrape and bow and apologize for it all and promise they'll *never* do it again—pah! Craven fools, the lot. No, I've heard far more than enough to make up my mind—"

He cut off suddenly with a grunt as he pitched forward on the deck, and I thought I heard his skull thump against the boards. Thomas bolted to his feet as Langford screamed, sliding astern as though something dragged him away.

I twisted, saw that something *was* dragging him, something with blazing red eyes. I thought the serpent had returned, but in a flash of lightning I saw Ginnie's face, her teeth now terrible fangs and the scales covering her entire upper body. Langford punched once, twice. Ginnie reared back and smashed her face into his, knocking him flat.

Charlotte was up now, screaming at the sight of her daughter. Jonnie, I saw, was senseless though his eyes gaped wide. Two punctures on his throat did not bleed.

The ship went dark. Another wave of nausea knocked me onto my back, and a cramp nearly doubled me over in my hammock.

I heard a faint hiss moving away: *"Senda mér hann!"*

Chapter 7

Thomas ran to Ginnie, quickly placing his hand on her shoulder as he spoke words of rebuke, but also comfort and hope. Charlotte sobbed as I shuffled, bent nearly double, to Jonnie under the Fire's compulsion on me. I placed one hand on his eyes, the other on his throat over the punctures as I sank into the Fire. I felt the spirit within him waning. It seemed battered by the same force battering Ginnie. *Even the captives of the mighty shall be taken away, and the prey of the terrible shall be delivered: for I will contend with him that contendeth with thee, and I will save thy children.*

The evil spirit slowed, and his own ebbed back. But I felt no blood pulse through him, no air moved through his lungs. *Surely he hath borne our griefs, and carried our sorrows: yet we did esteem him stricken, smitten of God, and afflicted. But he was wounded for our transgressions, he was bruised for our iniquities: the chastisement of our peace was upon him; and with his stripes we are healed.*

Jonnie's mouth twitched as though he longed to swallow, but could not. The seeing still had not returned to his eyes. *The light of the body is the eye: if therefore thine eye be single, thy whole body shall be full of light.*

He gasped, drew great lungfuls of air as the blood raced through him like a pent up river suddenly released. I helped him sit up, and Charlotte came to him—sobbing, still, but with relief behind it instead of fear or helpless guilt. Ginnie came over, too, her eyes returned to normal except the living fear behind them. Her skin still glowed with scales, though they seemed more a tattoo than true scales.

"And Langford?" I asked.

Thomas looked at me and shortly shook his head. Before I could press him he glanced suddenly toward the hatch.

"What is happening down here?" Captain Gavril's voice echoed from further forward. He held a lantern aloft, casting thin shadows in its orange glow.

I winced for how bright it seemed in our darkness. "Ginnie grows worse," I offered, assuming he knew from the ship's doctor of her original condition.

"I see." He came forward steadily, his sea legs sturdy as the ship continued to pitch. "I had not come to see her, but how is she?"

He was near enough, then, to see for himself. He froze, the lantern thrust forward in shock. "What is happening to her?" he whispered roughly.

I steadied myself against a beam. "I don't know," I said wearily. "She gets worse, then overcomes it. But it never goes away entirely."

"Perhaps we should talk separately," Thomas offered. I could tell by his tone that something had happened when he went to her.

I nodded toward my hammock, allowed Thomas to guide me there by my elbow. Gavril hesitated a moment longer before joining us, turning his back to block our voices.

"The spirit of Jörmungandr is in her," Thomas said as quietly as the wind and waves would allow. "I could feel him. Of more immediate concern, Captain, is Langford has been lost."

"Lost?" we both chorused.

Thomas nodded grimly. "I moved him further away, but some of your sailors should take his body out. It's astern, port side."

Gavril grimaced, but there was something else there I couldn't read. He glanced up and bellowed for one of his sailors: the man descended quickly and approached. I kept my eyes squeezed shut as he gave the orders. Thomas laid a hand on my forehead, murmuring words of the Fire. I felt as though he pushed back against a tide with a broom, though it did help a little.

"What is this about the spirit of that serpent?" Gavril murmured finally.

"He was assaulting Jonnie as well," I said. "But I think the power of Our Father was able to banish it." I clamped my mouth shut, gripping it with my hand as I swallowed against a retch. Thomas stroked my hair. "It had nearly overcome him, and I could tell it was the same as what came against Ginnie."

"I expect as much from twins," Thomas said. "Though he has a far stronger hold on young Ginnie. It is braided somehow with her spirit. Despite her fear of it, she holds on."

"Why?" I asked in horror.

"I think he's promising something that she wants, something secret," he said. "She is very much at war with herself over it."

I lifted my eyes to Gavril. "You know them as well, Captain," I said. "Do you know what he's talking about?"

"I cannot imagine it," he said. Again, I felt there was more behind his voice than his words. I gazed steadily at him until he finally lowered his eyes. "She is just a child. She cannot know what she wants—what it means to want it."

"Very likely true, Captain," I said. "And without the wisdom of her elders she will never know it."

He snorted, glancing appreciatively at me. "Perhaps you are a prophet," he murmured. "For you nearly strike upon it with those words." He scrubbed his jaw. "She's never forgiven her mother for having twins."

"She wants to be the eldest," I said. When he glanced sharply at me, I had to admit: "Charlotte told me."

"Hmm. Yes, and she clings to those few minutes as if they were years. But it would have been better if it had been years in truth."

"So if the Lindwurm can take Jonnie from her…"

But Thomas was shaking his head. "No, I think he promises to take Ginnie from her family," he said. "To be his only child, brought into the elder myths, the weight of ages behind her. She would be older than any of us, older than an entire race of people—at least in their mythologies."

I gaped. "But to become that—"

"She isn't given entirely to it, and probably he hasn't told her that specifically. Perhaps he only promises to take her somewhere that even those older than her would venerate her as an elder." He shrugged. "And then, even though she becomes more and more like the sea serpent, the lure of that promise drags on her."

I glanced back to where the mother and twins huddled. Jonnie was resting peacefully in Charlotte's arms again. And though her mother's left arm encircled her, Ginnie seemed less at peace. And suddenly her eyes locked onto mine and hardened, glittering in the Captain's lamplight as she considered us. They turned, watching as the sailors attempted discreetly to take Langford's body topside. The ghost of a smile came to Ginnie's lips, and the same instant I thought

I saw a bit of pink tongue pierce her lips, the sailors gasped in fear.

We all turned as Langford's body thumped to the deck and he cried out. "Where are you taking me?" he demanded. He sat up, rubbing the back of his head. "Ow, and why did you drop me?"

I turned to Thomas. He gaped at me, then at Gavril, clearly scrambling for an explanation. "Captain, I have seen dead men before—"

Gavril waved him off. "Stranger things have already happened on my ship," he said. He heaved a sigh. "And I thought I might have avoided it." He shook his head, frowning as though he chastised himself.

"What do you mean, Captain?" I asked. I felt a nudge, that I already knew where he was going. It was the next step in Saint Paul's tempestuous journey.

"The waves are filling the boat," he said. He glanced over as Langford approached. Gavril straightened, preparing himself for the argument. Langford saw it, and his hand dropped. They stared at each other, each reading the other's mind.

"You dare not," Langford growled.

"It is far better than drowning us all," Gavril retorted.

"It is the *same* as drowning us all," Langford said. "The entire purpose of this journey is getting this cargo to Algiers!"

"That purpose changed the moment this storm swept down on us," Gavril said. "Now our purpose is to get all these *souls* to Algiers, sir. Your cargo can be replaced."

"No, it cannot! Do you understand? There is nothing to replace it with—if this cargo is tossed into the sea, I am dead as surely as this boat sinking."

"We won't be," I said. I winced as my stomach pinched. "Forgive me," I said quickly. "I do not understand your circumstances. But you would consign the rest of us to death if you are not given the chance at life?"

His gaze bored into mine. "I thought you said we would make it without harm," he taunted. "Was that with, or without cargo?"

I smiled grimly. "There would be grievous hurt," I said. "But not death."

"Well, so much for Adloth, then?"

A hollow opened in my stomach, the winds of it battering the Flame. I didn't know. Perhaps by jumping off, he had already broken the prophecy. Was it possible?

"Our Father is not a man, that he should lie; neither the son of man, that he should repent: hath he said, and shall he not do it? or hath he spoken, and shall he not make it good?" Thomas said.

I blinked, then frowned. Before I could speak, though, Langford cut in. "Your Father is not real, either," he spat. "My cargo is real. And I promise you, Captain, by all the reality that I am—this cargo will not be cast overboard, or your life is forfeit." He spread his hands. "What is this crew worth? Your passengers? You ask the sacrifice of me: what of you? Will you throw yourself into the maw of the serpent to save us? Along with my cargo?"

Gavril's jaw tightened. "Very well, Langford," he said. "We'll ride it out a little while longer. Perhaps I'll have you lashed to your precious cargo so you can go to the bottom with it."

"An excellent idea, Captain!" he said brightly. "I will go to it now. And when you come for it, know you come for me as well."

He marched off, then deeper into the hold where his cargo had been stored. Gavril pounded a fist into his thigh. "The fool," he murmured, with more sorrow than anger, I felt.

"Why is it so precious to him?" I wondered.

Gavril sighed. "I do not think he spoke too far out of turn. As far as I know, if this cargo does not sell in Algiers, his master will hang him."

"The loss he mourned from a bad deal," I said, looking toward the black opening where Langford had disappeared below. "So he was telling the truth about his dream."

"I'm afraid he was. But I cannot imagine his master being so hard as to kill him if he offloaded it trying to save the ship."

I drew a breath and hiccuped. I shook my head, sinking into the Fire again. *What is this? Why am I fighting this sickness for so long?* It did not feel like a natural sickness. Too often it rose up at the height of some evil. *What am I missing?*

"You were about to say something, before Langford cut you off," Thomas said gently.

I ran my hand down his arm. "I was. Because you reminded me that Our Father carries out what He says. If that's true—wouldn't that mean that Adloth isn't dead?"

Both men stared at me. Gavril grinned first. "Normally I would say I know a dead man when I see one," he drawled.

Thomas flashed a grin, but sobered. "So if he isn't dead, but his body is not on board, where is he?"

I paused for one breath to consider my words. "In the belly of a great fish," I said.

Thomas considered me a long moment. "So do we have more than one Jonah?"

"No," I said quickly, before I threw up again. "No, the wrong one—" I almost said 'jumped off.' No more jumping off. "Confessed. Someone is still unrepentant."

Thomas glanced at Gavril. "Pretty much everyone has come through," he said.

I shook my head quickly. "It's not one of the crew. The serpent at the beginning wasn't around one of the crew—it was ashore, among the passengers. Probably it was already marking one of them."

Thomas frowned. "But it disappeared before Charlotte and the children arrived, didn't it? And yet it has clearly chosen Ginnie."

"But then again, when it was below, it moved through the passenger area," I countered. "There were still plenty of sailors to choose from."

"I would have thought, as a prophet of Our Father, you would be the one to tell us what we had done wrong and needed to repent of," Gavril said.

I considered the Fire, then bent my gaze on Thomas. I quirked an eyebrow, but he only shrugged slightly as he returned the expression. I winced as another stitch of nausea gripped me. "Maybe if it wasn't for the cursed sea," I muttered. Any time the Fire spoke, its words slid off my ear or bent around it. I could only hear faint snatches at times. *What is this? Why this chaos?*

They that go down to the sea in ships, that do business in great waters; these see the works of the LORD, and his wonders in the deep. For he commandeth, and raiseth the stormy wind, which lifteth up the waves thereof. They mount up to the heaven, they go down again to the depths: their soul is melted because of trouble. They reel to and fro, and stagger like a drunken man, and are at their wits' end. Then they cry unto the LORD in their trouble, and he bringeth them out of their distresses.

"Would many of your men pray, Captain?" I asked.

"I think they have already."

I smirked. It was worth a shot. Still... "Have you?"

He drew a breath, then looked up. He studied the planking for a moment, his eyes widening. "Excuse me," he said suddenly, dashing for the hatch.

I felt it then, too: the pitching was lessening. I stared at Thomas. "Surely not that easy," I said.

He shrugged again, then went toward the hatch. As he set one foot on a rung, suddenly the ship spun and lurched sideways. As my hammock swung wildly, I saw Thomas fall, his head thumping on the boards. There was a watery *BOOM* and the ship spun opposite. Planking groaned as the ship bucked. The twins awoke and began screaming; Charlotte joined them, I think out of motherly instinct alone. Feet stamped across the deck topside, incoherent orders were bellowed out, and five terrific cracks of thunder echoed so near I thought they must have hit the mast.

Sailors poured down the ladder like ants, scurrying further below. Mister Fields was close behind shouting about being stove in, to grab planks and ropes and pulleys. I could hear, faintly then, the sound of water as though pouring from some great spigot into a cavernous bucket. More shouts from below, as the twins' cries faded to sobs.

My mind spun, and what little I had in me threatened to come out again. I clamped my teeth against it. I allowed the tears to come, though. Endless days of frustration poured from heart to mind and back as I cried out against Our Father for putting us through this. *I'm done. I quit. Get us out of here, and leave me alone. Send someone else to do all this. If You love us at all, leave us alone on a farm somewhere, serving some other lord. I cannot do this! I cannot keep on, and I refuse to. If You require me to jump into the sea, then give me strength to get up to the deck and be done with it. I cannot.*

I dashed the tears away, looked up in time to see Thomas stagger to his feet. He paused only briefly to put a hand to the back of his head, then scurried up the ladder. I set my jaw. *Go. In vain, I'm sure. We're useless here. We did better work for the Kingdom in Fosse, and we were better fed and housed. But run, go see the endless waves. Try not to get struck by lightning. Or eaten by a serpent.* I folded my arms tight, waiting for the sound of Thomas' death by whatever means were conjured against us.

Movement caught my eye, and I saw Langford make his way up from below. The ship still rocked only a little, after the first several spins, and he moved listlessly to his hammock. He sat heavily, scrubbed his hair with his hands, and looked at me. I expected his gaze to harden, but then I thought perhaps he looked through me. He drew a heavy sigh, let his eyes continue to wander the deck.

I followed, saw Charlotte still huddled with the children. She was murmuring to them, some cradle-song or other:

Come, let us in sweet sleep
Drift away to sunlight.
Fields and clouds so bright,
In comfort broad and deep.
Carry us with your might.
We in thy bosom keep.
Let not our sin-cost reap
Your children; hold them tight.

I frowned. *Are you listening?* I asked petulantly. Langford met my gaze, and I could tell he looked at me now. His lip trembled, and I checked a sigh. *Am I listening?* "Is there much damage?" I asked softly. The storm had stilled enough, it was nearly silent in our compartment.

He held my gaze, then nodded. "I'm ruined," he said. "My lord is ruined. He will die in penury, now. And the best I could offer him is my own life, though it will change nothing."

"How does that happen?" I asked. "I confess ignorance in how merchanting works, despite traveling so long with Mahmoud. But I would think there is always a way to get more—"

I cut off as he shook his head. "No, another man had lent him money. Supposedly a friend, though I never felt safe with him. It was a very large sum." He drew a deep breath. "The terms of the loan were that he must be paid back promptly, for this friend had other investments he needed to cover. If not, my lord agreed to work from imprisonment until the loan could be repaid."

"You cannot work for it?" I asked.

His lip curled in a snarl. "I was not part of the terms."

I studied him a long moment. "It seems, indeed, that this 'friend' had hoped to beggar your lord," I said.

He shrugged. "My lord did not have to entrust me with the cargo, though. That was his own folly."

"What will you do?" I asked.

"It is not a total loss, not yet," he said. "I will sell what I can—who knows, maybe the markets will be good to me. Of course, I have to make it there first. With my cargo."

My stomach had eased, and I turned again to the Fire. *I'm sorry. I need your help, though. I was not lying when I said I could not do this anymore. But I need hope. And if I do, this crew does as well.*

"*Our Father hath given thee all them that sail with thee,*" I repeated. As soon as I said it, I waited for some other catastrophe to hit the ship. I held my breath, and I think Langford did as well.

"You said something similar before," he said, as though reading my thoughts.

I blinked in the silence and darkness, took a steadying breath. Then another. "Hmph." I sat up, stood upon the deck. When I glanced around, I saw everyone's eyes on me.

My nausea had shrunk to a little ball of iron, and the Fire roared merrily within.

Chapter 8

It first took me to the ladder, then topside. The rain still fell, but the waves were keeping their distance as though we rested a moment within a giant watery bowl. At that distance, the waves still rose to staggering heights, and I swallowed uncertainly. But the Fire called to me: for now, we were at peace.

Thomas, I saw, was nearer the bow with Mahmoud and Khalid, heads down in conversation. Thomas gestured toward me, then looked and actually saw me. He straightened, his brow furrowed.

I took a deep breath of the sea air, the first since we had set sail. Salty but pure, it carried none of the rotting, stagnant scents I had so detested at the wharf. I took another breath. There was an energy in the air that seeped into my spirit, bracing me for something. As if I waited with expectancy, yet distant enough I was skeptical of that expectation's fulfillment. I waited there a moment, feeling it out—or perhaps, feeling my way toward something. But I knew not where I was going, or why, and so I returned to the Fire's warm embrace.

Thomas appeared to be finishing his conversation. I sensed it was right. I surveyed the deck. One of the masts had broken: the large *boom* I had heard below. It was secured against the bulkhead now. The torches hissed and spat, but burned. Inexorably, I turned my head toward Adloth's flaming visage.

Though he writhed and screamed in silence, it was less intense than when he had first appeared, as though he had tired himself out. His screams would pause every now and again as his eyes cast about, looking for something. I approached, the Fire in me reaching out toward him. I paused directly at it, studied the blue flame, studied him. I was able to look into his eyes in ways I had not before, while he was alive and in front of me. Saw in them an anguish not borne of external punishment. He loathed himself for something, saw in whatever punishment he was facing that he was the direct cause of it. So I thought, perhaps, he was in no actual physical pain. If he was in the serpent's belly, as I strongly suspected, it was not digesting him.

I reached out my hand—my former, cursed, left hand—and held it near the blue flame. As in Holden, it did not burn. But now, rather than entering me, my Fire entered it. *I cried by reason of mine affliction unto the LORD, and he heard me; out of the belly of hell cried I, and thou heardest my voice.*

His writhing paused, though he still sobbed. He would have been gasping, I felt, if he were on deck. But he was listening.

The waters compassed me about, even to the soul: the depth closed me round about, the weeds were wrapped about my head. I went down to the bottoms of the mountains; the earth with her bars was about me for ever: yet hast thou brought up my life from corruption, O LORD my God.

His mouth closed, set somewhat. His eyes darted in fear, but he was calming. I plunged my hand completely into the flame, pressed my palm against his forehead. *When my soul fainted within me I remembered the LORD: and my prayer came in unto thee, into thine holy temple. Then I said, I am cast out of thy sight; yet I will look again toward thy holy temple.*

He took a breath, but pulled away from my hand. I drew it back, considering him. He turned aside, his jaw still set. I frowned, placed a finger to my lips. I had delivered to him what he needed, hadn't I? Was his position not precisely the same? And I did not feel sick again, so surely I had not misspoken.

And when he sowed, some seeds fell by the way side, and the fowls came and devoured them up.

"Hmm," I hummed to myself, then turned to the stern. The helmsman looked away: clearly he had been staring at me, and returned his gaze to the direction of the ship. I smiled, until my eyes were inevitably drawn to the Lindwurm still coiling in our wake.

And what do I have for you? I wondered. I made my way aft, up the steps to the quarter deck. I stood near the railing, but not braced against it. My sea legs had apparently found me—or, the Fire inside steadied me so surely amidst this storm. I gazed upon the serpent, studied it. Waiting, I think, for it to say something.

It studied me in return. I felt it smiled, though it might have simply been the serpentine shape of its lips. And yet it showed no fear, no pride or arrogance, no humor otherwise. No malice, I realized. It simply was. A fact of the sea, and it knew it. It needed to prove nothing to me or anyone else. Did not need to humble me with some display of power or control. It might have been another storm cloud, except for the dazzling display of its shimmering white scales, the scarlet of its tongue as it now and then waved in the air.

It rode the waters as steady as I stood, the coils of its body rolling endlessly in and out of the waves while the neck arched, but tall and unwavering as a fir. The glowing red eyes gazed at me. Finally I felt the slightest wave of dark fear roll from it, feeling its way around me. *You should have listened to me.*

I cocked my head. *We ought to obey Our Father rather than men.*

Who do you think sent me?

I paused again in thought. Could it be? Again the story of Jonah came to mind. In it, Our Father had prepared a fish for him, to swallow him. It was a place, eventually, to teach Jonah repentance and to spit him from sea back to land where he was supposed to be. Was this Lindwurm here to do His will? *Why has he sent you?* I thought. *And for whom?*

I am an agent of His wrath, to mete out against his enemies what they deserve.

I frowned. *Ye do err, not knowing the scriptures, nor the power of Our Father. But the heavens and the earth, which are now, by the same word are kept in store, reserved unto fire against the day of judgment and perdition of ungodly men. The Beloved is not slack concerning his promise, as some men count slackness; but is longsuffering to us-ward, not willing that any should perish, but that all should come to repentance.*

The coils writhed a little faster, the froth of the sea churned a little more. *You would keep me from my appointed duty? And how did the little one fare when you intervened in her dreams?* Now I could promise it smiled at me, a condescending grin as though it chided me. *Would allowing her dreams to be touched be so much worse compared to her injuries now?* The head lowered, the eyes brightening as they pierced me. *Stop meddling in what you do not understand, little child. Stop trying to hinder me, before my wrath is loosed without restraint.*

I heard footsteps, and Thomas was beside me. "Having a good conversation?" he asked. Though his tone was light, it also told me he knew what was going on. Had maybe even heard the both of us, somehow.

I saw the eyes shift, the smile harden. *Ah, the youngling's master.* Thomas' eyebrows shot skyward. *Well, aren't you?*

"*But for Adam there was not found an help meet for him. The rib, which Our Father had taken from man, made he a woman. Therefore shall a man cleave unto his wife: and they shall be one flesh,*" Thomas replied.

But is not the man the head of the wife?

Thomas laughed. "Ask my head how it would fare without my body, or my body without my head. Or ask my head whether it is master only, or if it has any control over a broken body. My *helper*," he continued with emphasis, "has been sick of body most of this voyage. Her head was no more 'master' of it, just because it was the head, than I would be of her. Even if I wanted to."

I spared him a glance. I still had not determined why I was so sick, and part of me wished he had not broached the subject. Returning to the Lindwurm, he had suddenly lowered his head, brought it near the stern. *Do you think she cannot hear us both?*

Thomas folded his arms. "Perhaps the crew needs to hear the words of Our Father as well."

My insides trembled as the Fire lanced through me. The rain fell harder and colder, and the Lindwurm's smile became terrible. "As you wish," he said. His voice was fire and smoke and ash, gravel and earth, roaring through a fertile valley to its utter ruin. "I will say all again: I am sent by your father to bring wrath and punishment upon this ship, upon certain of its cargo. I will not leave, and this storm will not cease, until I depart with what I came for. And with whom."

Thomas faltered not a whit. "I will not tolerate lies," he said. "This ship and its cargo will make this passage safely. I'm afraid you have the wrong boat."

The smile disappeared as suddenly as it had widened. "Do you want to tempt me—the agent of your Father's wrath?"

Thomas' brows rose again. "Tempt you?" he repeated. "*Our Father cannot be tempted with evil, neither tempteth he any man.*"

"I am not your father!" the Lindwurm roared.

I nearly expected fire to come out and burn us all. But Thomas was right, and I stared keenly at the beast. "That, we can tell," I said. "And neither are you his agent, I suspect. Where do you truly come from?"

His eyes lit on me, and I saw the rage nearly un-bound in them. I worried we had pushed too far, too fast. Many of our other opponents had been reduced before we engaged them so boldly. Perhaps that time was past. But perhaps not.

Quick feet pattered up behind us, and Robert was suddenly at the railing. "Forgive them," he sputtered. The Lindwurms' gaze shifted to him. "They are young, as you said. Quick-tempered. And too quick of mouth," he said, casting a sharp glance at us. "They forget to be quicker to hear. Tell us, then, who it is you have been sent for. If we can, we will give them up."

The Lindwurm stared at him for a time as though considering. Finally he looked once more at us. "Does he speak for this ship?"

"I offer my opinion," Robert said. "Hopefully, before these two consign us all to the depths. At least tell us who Our Father is angry with."

The Lindwurm glowered, then drew back. "Hear this, ship of fools," he trumpeted. "Even now a fire burns in some of you. Even now some of you are overgrown in your hearts, nearly swallowed by the malignant growth in you. If you would spare this ship, cast yourselves in. One has made the right choice." I looked back at Adloth, saw his eyes squeezed shut against the Lindwurm's blasts. "Two more are due me." His fiery gaze took in both Thomas and I. "Choose soon, before this storm chooses for you. For if it does, you will all come to me."

He drew back to his customary distance, and I felt a sealing off, knew the conversation was over. I looked at Robert, his knuckles white on the railing. He shifted to look sideways at the two of us, a rage of similar nature if not in timbre to the Lindwurm's. "It's you two, isn't it?" he seethed.

"Us?" Thomas said before I could.

"Of course! Who else? Who was so bold as to claim a fire and some growing seed? Who else reacts so strongly to the actions of this serpent? And who else keeps shoving blame off on everyone else, redirecting pertinent questions with questionable quotes—the Sacred Words twisted for their own use and control?"

"Control?" Thomas echoed. "We've spoken words of comfort, as they've been given to us. I don't remember trying to control anyone."

"Ah yes, comfort," Robert mocked. "'Don't throw anyone off the ship—especially not us. We'll all be fine so long as we all stay on board' Ha!" he spat. "A fine way to keep yourselves on board while those who know no better fling themselves off in an ultimately doomed sacrifice. Look on him!" he continued, his voice rising as his finger flung at Adloth. "He hoped to save us, and now writhes in endless despair because of your lies."

"You take this from the words of the Lindwurm?" I asked.

"I take it as logical," he returned. "And yes, what he says makes sense."

"And yet you try to throw guilt on us as though Adloth innocently sacrificed himself, when the Wurm said Adloth was due him." I waited for Robert to swallow, but not to continue his speech. "I made an error," I continued hurriedly, "in naming the prophet Jonah. I don't know why it came to me, but it did. Even so, I spoke out of turn—and yes, Adloth perhaps suffers because of it. And perhaps that was why I have been sick until now. But if you'll look, he is not in as much pain as he was." I watched Robert's eyes as he looked, knew I was right as his features changed. "Further, I do not believe he is dead. I was promised none would die on this voyage, and I do not believe Our Father has gone back on His promise, or that His word has been thwarted."

Gavril took a step toward us. "On what assurances?"

"Several. *God is not a man, that he should lie; neither the son of man, that he should repent: hath he said, and shall he not do it? or hath he spoken, and shall he not make it good?* And *For we walk by faith, not by sight.* By all accounts of our sight, Langford had died by a serpent's hand belowdecks—yet suddenly he came back to life. Why?" I paused, seeing the crew frozen on deck as they listened. "Except for the promise of Our Father, and the lies of this serpent. Great damage has been done to the ship, yet it still floats—because the time is not yet right for us to be free of this storm." The Captain grimaced, but held his peace. I wondered if the damage was less severe than I thought, but I continued. "There is something yet to be confessed on this ship—perhaps by us, perhaps by others. But freedom will not come by abandoning this ship."

"You meddle in things you don't understand," Robert said, clearly unconvinced.

"The Lindwurm said much the same," I countered.

He barked a frustrated shout. "You don't even call him by the right name! Will you all truly listen to this witless chit? Will you hang your life on her uneducated words?"

My arm went out automatically, before I heard Thomas' step, halting him. "*Now when they perceived that they were unlearned and ignorant men, they marvelled; and they took knowledge of them, that they had been with The Beloved.*" I said. "By our fruit you will know us.

Tell me, Robert, from which fruit of the Spirit do your words come? Love? Peace? Kindness?"

"Righteous indignation," he said. "At those who would take the name of Our Father in vain, using it for selfish gain."

I quirked a half-smile. "I'm unfamiliar with that fruit. But also, we must be quite certain of our chances of survival if this ship sinks."

"You probably made a deal with the serpent."

"I would ask not only how, but why," I said.

"Oh, not before the voyage. Once we were all on board. You offered that poor little girl instead of yourself as thrall, the night its offspring disturbed their dreams. Now in return for the rest of our lives, it will carry you to safety once we're all dead."

My heart sank, because I could think of no way to contradict him. We could certainly not prove him wrong, and I saw no obvious flaw in his reasoning, beyond the fact it wasn't true.

"That is…an impressive line of reasoning," Gavril said behind us. I glanced at him, worried. But a tongue of Fire leaped up inside, drawing me down into its comfort, and I waited. "Unfortunately," the Captain continued, "I see absolutely nothing in their character to uphold such an idea. I have heard reports of my men—whom I trust far more than you, worthy monk—of their care and concern for all aboard this vessel."

"I am a man of Our Father!" Robert spluttered.

"So are they," Gavril countered easily. "And as Rae-Anna said, by your fruits you will be known. I order no one to jump off this ship, as we are far from stove-in just yet. Not only because of the words Rae-Anna and Thomas have spoken, but on my own honor to carry you all safely to Algiers. I wish no loss of life or needless sacrifice."

Robert's teeth ground together, but before he could say anything, the winds rose again, moaning through the rigging. Gavril turned swiftly, and all our gazes swung to the fore as the waves—beforehand a distant wall—were swiftly approaching once more.

"Clear the decks!" Gavril shouted. "My sailors alone on the lines—all passengers below until I say!"

We hurried to obey, barely making it down the hatch before the first wave broke over the railing. Seawater splattered on us all, running nearly to our ankles as the ship bucked. We made our way aft to our hammocks. Charlotte and the twins gazed at us with wide eyes.

"The reprieve is over," I said as the wind howled above. I all but fell into my hammock as the stern pitched up. Others toppled into theirs as it came back down.

I glanced over, saw Langford lying stiffly on his hammock, eyes squeezed shut. I thought I saw a tear leak down the side of his face, but there was water everywhere. I looked back at Ginnie, at the strange scales glistening in the occasional flash of lightning as the thunder resumed its steady percussions.

Come ye yourselves apart into a desert place, and rest a while.

I looked at Thomas, whose gaze told me he had received much the same. I didn't see how we could, but I understood the need. We had been given much to ponder. As I lay back, I spared one final glance toward Robert, whose eyes glittered as he stared at us. Gavril had clearly not convinced him, or at least had not changed his mind. *Father, protect us,* I prayed, though in truth it felt unnecessary. And yet the Fire glowed within, and as I stayed in prayer, the sounds of the storm and the ship quieted away, and I was borne away in warmth and providence, Fire and Seed side by side.

Chapter 9

We drifted together through vast expanses, among the starry host, down winding rivers to plunging waterfalls, resting at times and wandering at others. We came at last to a pool still as a mirror, a single snow-capped peak in the distance. Deer browsed against a backdrop of firs, and an eagle glided overhead. I lay in the pool, Thomas beside me, communing with Our Father in the splendor of His creation. I felt more than saw His indelible mark in every aspect, tainted though it was with the Liar's attempts to bring everything under his dominion. In that stillness I began to see somewhat of Our Father's designs. I saw also the Liar's war he brought against it, saw his points of advance, saw what he defended in bulwark. But it was all distantly; here in this pool beside this mountain was only rest. Solitude, yet filled with presence. An escape from the violent seas I remembered our little ship drifted on. But also in that rest, in that solitude, was a recharging energy. The war was not over, and we were drawn away only to be sent back in greater strength, with better knowledge and understanding. To rest, to escape, without that would have been time wasted. And Our Father required all the resources we had in and through Him.

And so, when we ran out again from that pool, I did not mourn or wish to stay longer. There were souls out there in bondage and torment. Souls who might never experience that rest and solitude except we brought them to The Beloved, who could carry them here. So Fire and Seed went on, fueled and fueling, across the mountain towards storm clouds, an ocean drenched by rains and tossed by winds. And with us we carried a tiny pocket of peace like leaven.

I blinked open my eyes as thunder crashed, gripping the hammock as the stern dropped beneath us. There was a momentary lurch in my throat and I blinked harder. I looked at Thomas.

Back to His work.

I sat up, looked around the passenger quarters. The low deck and the darkness weighed on me in equal parts to that far mountain and sky had lifted me up. Someone coughed. Rain and wind raged as rigging creaked. Charlotte was murmuring again, a different cradle song I could not hear.

I moved to her, sat nearby. She looked at me with glistening eyes as she rocked Ginnie in their hammock. The girl was poised, eyes fixed ahead. At least they were not red. But her silvery scales like tattoos were still painfully evident.

Jonnie sat up, blinking around. His eyes lit on me, sitting on the deck, and he got up and came to me. I swallowed my surprise as he sat with me, leaned into the arm I offered. I picked up the tune of Charlotte's song and mimicked it for him. And for a time we sat just so.

"Stop, mother," Ginnie said suddenly. "I'm not a child anymore."

The song died abruptly as a tear slid down Charlotte's cheek. And yet Ginnie had not moved from her spot. I expected her to get up, or try to. That fact struck me peculiarly.

"Are you not a child?" I asked gently. "And why shouldn't you be?"

Her eyes met mine. "I'm not some silly girl. I'm almost of marrying age."

I let a small grin quirk my lips. "Are you eager for that?"

Her gaze drifted away again. "Eagerness doesn't matter. It will be my duty."

"Oh, but not yet Ginnie," Charlotte cried. "Why should you say so? Don't let duty fall on you too soon." She rested her chin on Ginnie's shoulder, but Ginnie shrugged it off forcefully.

"I said stop that," she said. "Someone must be responsible. Someone must do what has to be done, with or without eagerness. Life demands it."

"It doesn't have to be you—not so young!"

Ginnie looked away to the left. "Who will: you?" she asked scornfully. "Jonnie?" Her eyes fixed on me next, as though challenging me specifically though she did not say so.

"Your mother has watched over you dutifully this whole storm," I offered.

She grinned viciously. "And who brought us into this storm to begin with?"

I glanced at Charlotte as more tears streamed silently down her cheeks. "This is not the first voyage she has brought you on."

Ginnie snorted. "Of course not. All she wants to do is sail. Any excuse she can make up to get us on a boat to somewhere else. I'm sure she would have rather not given us birth."

"Oh Ginnie, that's not true! I never—of course, I...but, it's not like..." She faltered into silence, squeezing her eyes shut as she shook her head.

Ginnie continued to fix me with her gaze. "Of course she wanted something different, but it's not like she had a choice," she said, as though filling in the words her mother was afraid to speak. "So she tells everyone, anyway, when she thinks I can't hear. Not that I need to hear it: I can tell by the way we get dragged everywhere with her."

"I like sailing with her," Jonnie said quietly.

Ginnie's gaze flickered to him. "You're still a child," she spat. "Little baby Jonnie, can't think for himself yet."

"It's fun," he said. "You just don't have fun anymore."

Her jaw clenched, and she held up her arms covered in scales. "Fun."

Jonnie turned his head further into me, and she dropped her arms as she stared at me again. "Was that fun?" she asked, her eyes glancing across my face.

I snorted a laugh. "Of course not. It wasn't duty either. Nor do I stop having fun just because the Liar's agents marked my flesh."

"And when you were sick in this storm? Was that fun, too?"

I studied her a moment. "For someone consumed with duty, you also are very concerned with whether something is fun, or not fun."

She grumped, looked away and back. "You're the one telling me to *have* fun."

"We're telling you to find joy and happiness where you can," I countered. "Life will offer enough times when you must be responsible, and times when you must take your duties seriously. Don't chase those times. *For I have learned, in whatsoever state I am, therewith to be content.* Though," I amended, "I personally am still learning."

"And did your mother drag you throughout her life?"

I smiled thinly. "My mother kicked me out of her home when I was not much older than you," I said. I lifted my arm from Jonnie's shoulder. "Left handed."

I heard a grunt from elsewhere, glanced around to see a sailor who had come below pausing as though in mid-stride. His eyes took us all in. And I thought, for a moment, they flashed red—though, blue lightning flashed at that very moment, too. When the darkness returned he went quickly back up the ladder. I frowned, nearly made a comment when I noticed Robert glaring at me, mild horror in his gaze.

"Sinister?" he growled. Even Charlotte now considered me with apprehension.

"The Sisters of the Convent in Holden declared me not-cursed," I assured them. "And The Sacred Fire in me comforted me long before they did." I returned to Ginnie. "And The Beloved has since then 'dragged' me continually southward. It is not always fun, and I have known fear almost as much as I have known happiness. I resist the first with the power of The Beloved, and rejoice in the other as often as it is available."

Ginnie frowned, but made no response. I thought, perhaps, her skin pinked a little. It was difficult to tell amidst the darkness and my earnest hope. We sat in this repose for long moments more, and I felt Jonnie drifting away again. My legs were growing stiff in their curled position, so I lifted him gently up, stood, and helped him into his hammock. I stretched, knuckling my back.

Thomas, I saw, was sitting with Mahmoud. Khalid was nearby, and though he lay quietly, it seemed to me as though his ears pricked. I glanced around for Agnarr. I could not recall seeing him for some time now. His berth was empty, and I could not miss his bulk—compressed as it would be. Perhaps he was still topside, where he was more comfortable.

Robert's gaze again caught my attention, and I returned to my hammock near his. He watched me settle myself in. I stared pointedly at him, waiting for him to say whatever was clearly on his mind.

Finally he drew a breath.

"So, you were under the guidance of Sisters for part of your life?"

"I was."

"You should have stayed."

I shrugged. "They did not think so."

He arched an eyebrow. "And did you convince them of that?"

I blinked, casting back in my mind. "I argued my position," I said slowly. "But I think it was the Holy Words that convinced them."

He huffed, staring at me with a mix of anger, frustration, and—I thought—desperate curiosity. "And you are so sure you know what those are? Without being taught?"

I arched my brows. "Only rarely," I said. He blinked, frowning. I couldn't help but laugh. "Certainly I know it is Our Father who brings them to me. What they always mean?" I shook my head. "He often must beat me over the head with it before I understand. Take this serpent: I would not be surprised if He has already given me all the knowledge I need to understand. It's getting past whatever still blinds me that's delaying it."

"It might also be up to someone else," he said.

"Hmm. Could be," I said, genuinely surprised by the idea. "We do all like to be the protagonists in our stories, don't we?"

He granted me a brief smile, I could not tell how genuine. "Our Father is the protagonist in them all."

I hummed again. "Ultimately, yes. But in the Holy Words He still tells the story through certain individuals, doesn't he?" Robert nodded begrudgingly. "And of course we all want ourselves to be that certain individual. In small parts, we may be. Maybe even for those on this ship, one or the other of us will be the lead character when they retell this tale. Do you think?"

"I try not to," he said. "It tends toward pride."

I nodded with a sigh. "Yes, I'm afraid I fell into that already. Blessed are we that Our Father's plans are not so easily thwarted. I wonder, though, what makes a protagonist? Is it the one through whom change comes?"

"We are speaking strictly of the stories we tell each other?" he asked. I nodded. He shrugged. "It is the one without whom the story does not finish."

"Hmm. And why is he, or she, the one that becomes so central to the story? Is it simply because everything the story requires happens to them?"

He considered a moment. "No," he said eventually. "Things happen to everyone. But they make decisions, and take actions, that impact and eventually lead to the end."

"They are obedient to bring the change necessary," I said.

He studied me as though he sought a flaw. "What, if so?"

"Does our obedience to Our Father bring change?"

"It should, I suppose."

"So we might all be protagonists in the story He is telling through us."

"Ah," he said, lifting a finger. "But His story might not be being told through us."

"How do you mean."

"It is His story to tell, not ours. We might be obedient to our parts, but it does not automatically make us the protagonist. The question is whether you are in total submission to whatever He needs you to be. Would you be one of the daughters of Job?"

"One of those who died, you mean," I said.

He nodded. "Our Father revealed Himself to the Patient Sufferer only after he suffered. Do you think his children thought they were the lead characters in their stories? And yet what point did they serve but to teach us all, eventually, of the supremacy of Our Father? What change they brought, if any, was only in how their father reacted to their deaths."

"*For we which live are alway delivered unto death for The Beloved's sake, that the life also of The Beloved might be made manifest in our mortal flesh,*" I said. "And giving up our life does not always mean the death of our mortal bodies. So I suppose I'm saying I agree with you," I went on with a smile. "We have died so the glorious story of Our Father might be revealed to those who still suffer. We are already Job's children, aren't we."

Robert sat back, folding his arms. "I will have to ask the Brothers when I reach Algiers," he said.

I barely kept the sigh from escaping my lips. "It would be interesting to know what they say," I said instead. "Will they tell you where to go next?" I asked, suddenly wondering.

"I assume so," he replied easily. "As the Fire directs me, surely it directs them as well, so we *may with one mind and one mouth glorify Our Father, even the Father of The Beloved.*"

"So you felt no specific direction at first?" I asked. "Just, what? A warming toward the will of the Brothers in Chantereaux?"

He stared blankly at me for a moment. "Oh! Them. Yes—well, something like that. I perhaps felt...well, does it matter? I went to them, and they directed me."

I frowned, wondering what he was about to admit feeling. But Thomas and Mahmoud approached just then; Thomas sat with me, Mahmoud on Thomas' hammock, both looking at me expectantly. "Yes?" I asked.

"We've been speaking with Khalid," Thomas said.

I nodded. "I noticed. Is he all right?"

Thomas rubbed his palms on his thighs. "No. Mahmoud told him about what you had done for him in Holden. The healing?" I nodded again, quickly. "Well. Khalid thinks you stole Mahmoud from Azrael. That Jörmungandr is here for him—Mahmoud," he clarified with a gesture. "And he's the one who should jump from the ship."

I rolled my eyes. "Azrael is the angel of death?" I asked. Mahmoud nodded. "A fairly weak angel? Easily thwarted by young women?" I glanced behind him to where Khalid lay in his hammock, turned resolutely away.

"He is not to be taken lightly," Mahmoud said.

"Did he threaten you?" I asked, my brows rising.

"I did not mean Khalid; Azrael," Mahmoud replied.

"Hmm. I guess I'm not trying to. I don't know much about him. But I would think, being an angel, he could handle his own. Azrael, that is." I shook my head again.

"Khalid did threaten you, though," Thomas said quietly.

I glanced between them, but Mahmoud was shaking his head. "He speaks big words," he said. "I have not been away from Algiers so long as he thinks I have. He has little power."

"What did he threaten to do?"

Mahmoud began to protest again, but Thomas cut him off. "Khalid said he would prevent Mahmoud from trading any of his goods. That his name would be marked out of the rolls, and he would find no buyer or seller in any market in Ifriqiya. And neither would his wife, or any of his family."

Mahmoud made a disgusted sound. "I wish to be there when Khalid tries to keep my wife from trading her goods," he growled.

I gave a half-smile, but Thomas still seemed troubled. "What is it?" I asked.

"I'm not sure. I understand Mahmoud's skepticism, but Khalid seemed quite certain. And he was loose with his threat—said everyone on board would find no luck or welcome after we landed."

I frowned. "I'm siding with Mahmoud more and more. How would Khalid possibly accomplish that? He cannot get messages there before we land, and won't he—"

"Ah, I think he can," Thomas cut in. "If this storm lifts, and apparently he is sure it will, he has a messenger bird he promises to send immediately."

I pursed my lips, glancing at Mahmoud. "Despite your own feelings, and no disrespect to the competency of your wife and her family," I said; "is it at all possible Khalid is that well connected?"

Mahmoud glowered. "If he has become so, it is because he is underhanded, sly, and a thief," he spat. "And surely we can prove him, and cut out his support."

"How long would that take?" I asked.

Mahmoud folded his arms, but said nothing. Langford rose, looked at us all. "Need to use the, uh...you know." He trailed off, and made his way to the hatch. I scrubbed my forehead.

"You wish me to obey him?" Mahmoud asked.

I looked scornfully at him. "Of course not. I'm just wondering how much trouble we'll be sailing into, provided we sail out of our current trouble." Formerly, we only needed to deal with one crisis at a time—only knew about one at a time, and only when it was already upon us. Now suddenly it seemed we might start planning for the next, with no rest. And to think Ginnie longed for the duties of being an adult. *Enjoy it while you can, for all of our sakes.* I glanced back to Charlotte and the twins, startling as I saw Ginnie staring at me. A red tongue flicked out, and her eyes flashed briefly red as she grinned.

My eyes widened. "Thomas—Langford!"

He stared, and we bolted toward the hatch at the same time. I let Thomas precede me, and as my head neared the opening, I thought I heard Ginnie giggling. The storm crashed around us, and I searched frantically around, futilely wiping rain from my face.

"Forward! He's—no!" Thomas shouted. I looked ahead as Langford stepped off the railing, my breath catching in my throat until I heard, faintly, the splash of him hitting the water.

I whirled, saw the Lindwurm loop his head underwater, then rise again. Crimson seawater drained from his mouth as he grinned, his eyes fixed on me.

"One more," he said, his voice of gravel and ash squishing now as it murmured across the waves.

All aboard, including me, stared at him as he returned calmly to his trailing posture. The coils rolled as the waves did, his neck like a mast barely even bobbing. His eyes fixed on us, but with a hunger that was not desperate. He knew, eventually, more would jump off in hopes of saving the ship. He as much as promised it in the hearing of all.

"Rae-Anna," Thomas said quietly. I looked at him, followed his finger where he pointed. Langford was in the flames of the torch next to Adloth's, his face a mask of sorrow and terror. Adloth's head now bent in defeat, wagging slowly as though he sobbed without hope.

I found I could relate to him, as the storm continued to beat against the boat.

Chapter 10

The mood belowdecks I could only describe as numb. The storm raged, and raged, and faded now almost to the background. I knew, if we made it through, the ground would feel foreign for not constantly moving up and down. Water tumbled down the hatch, slid across the deck, and down another hatch into the hold. I spent a few moments contemplating Langford's cargo, which he must have counted as completely lost. I berated myself for being so callous in our conversations. For his part, Langford must have taken Khalid's threat seriously, and any feeble candle of hope he had retained was snuffed.

But I could not care too long. My emotions had frayed, then thinned, and now were gone. The Fire inside was a pale tongue, without warmth, burning as through frosted glass on a winter day. Thomas and I, from time to time, would gaze at each other. But we could not speak, could not begin to form into words the helplessness and hopelessness that was simply a hole inside us. I truly believe now that without that moment of rest under that mountain, we might have tossed ourselves overboard as well. Even with the memory of that experience, I'm not sure how we didn't.

Why? You said You would, and so far You have not. You know we cannot go on without You, and yet You draw back when You promised to come forward. What have we done wrong? What do we need to do?

Oh, Our Father, where are you?

Perhaps, if I had remembered that this part of our journey displayed bits of prophecy, I would not have prayed so. Perhaps it was unrelated. But, I get ahead of us.

In the moment, I felt utterly betrayed. The Father I thought I relied on showed Himself unreliable, at least to my expectations. Nothing worked, nothing changed anything, no amount of investigation or love or compassion or truth mattered. There was the storm, and the Lindwurm, and people devoured.

Gradually, I registered that each time water came through the hatch, it sounded louder and poured longer. But in my inexperience and my numbness it meant nothing until Captain Gavril came below. I gazed at him. He took a step or two forward as other sailors descended behind him. Those continued to the next ladder as Gavril only looked at me, silent and a little grim.

"What is it?" I asked finally.

"The waters are still high," he said. He took another half-step forward just as water crashed to the deck behind him. "We have to lighten the ship."

It still took a few moments for it to make sense, and only made the connection as the first group of sailors appeared again with one of Langford's crates of goods between them. I sat up in consternation, but despair hit me again before I could protest. What else was he to do? He had said this was necessary when Langford still resided on the ship. Now that he was gone...

"You know we believe he still lives, somewhere," I said.

"If he does, he may be in a far safer place than us," Gavril said. "And if he returns, he will be as free as the rest of us to make our fortunes as we can."

"Did daddy approve this?" Charlotte spoke up.

Gavril set his jaw, clasped his hands tightly behind him. "Master Kingsley asked me to extend his deepest apologies and torments, that this ship has held up so poorly."

There was a spark in the Captain's eye that attuned the Fire in me. "This ship has held up far better than any other you've captained, hasn't it?" I asked.

He fixed me with his gaze. "I would not openly contradict Master Kingsley."

I nodded, respecting his position. I watched another two sailors make their way topside with more goods. Curious, I turned to look at Ginnie. But she had no regard for the proceedings, nestling instead close to her brother. The scales were unchanged on her. Still, I had to assume the Lindwurm truly had no interest in the boat itself. Otherwise, I expected that he, through Ginnie, would be gloating. Any damage or loss must be secondary.

Gavril stepped closer. "You did warn us, didn't you," he said.

My gaze focused. "I suppose I did. But the rest still stands: we will all make it through alive."

"Why, do you suppose, that is?"

"Because I was promised—"

He shook his head. "Not that. Why press us, only to spare us?"

I grinned, though weakly, remembering Aurden. *Every branch that beareth fruit, he purgeth it, that it may bring forth more fruit.* Grape vines must be pruned, anything extra taken away, to make room for fruitful growth. I cannot imagine lopping off those vines is pleasant to the plant, if they had feelings."

"Do you believe, then, that off-loading these goods will appease Jörmungandr? Is that what he seeks?"

I paused, glancing at Thomas. His gaze mirrored my thoughts. "No," I said finally. "There is more to come. But this may preserve us a little longer, to make it through whatever is coming."

I could tell it was not what he wanted to hear, and after a moment he turned on his heel, bellowing to the sailors to make way as he ascended topside again. I sighed, my gaze forlorn at Thomas. *"How beautiful upon the mountains are the feet of him that bringeth good tidings, that publisheth peace; that bringeth good tidings of good, that publisheth salvation; that saith unto Zion, Thy God reigneth!"*

Thomas grinned crookedly. *"There is yet one by whom we may enquire of Our Father: but I hate him; for he doth not prophesy good concerning me, but evil."*

I snorted a laugh. "Our Father truly thought of everything when He gave us the Holy Words, didn't he?" I said.

Thomas cocked an eyebrow as he sobered. "I guess He had to. My Seed and your Fire are comforts, to be sure. But too easy to neglect, or dismiss as our own wishful thinking. But when all else can be ignored, the Words are there."

"An anchor in the storm," I murmured. I listened to the rain pounding the deck, the grunts of the sailors maneuvering cargo topside. "I keep thinking back to Holden," I continued. "Some of the grand speeches I made. And I'm worried I overstepped my bounds. Or, that the message I delivered was meant more for me than them."

Thomas grunted. "I don't agree."

I lifted a shoulder. "Well, in the moment I didn't either. And I felt it was the prompting of the Sacred Fire, every syllable. And yet—did I dismiss the Sisters too readily? What they stood for, or believed in? We just said how important the Holy Words are, something stable when our emotions or senses are in a whirl. But back there I assumed, and spoke as if, the whirl was exactly where we should be."

"Well, I mean, here we are," Thomas said. His words were punctuated by a lurching drop toward the stern.

I grinned appreciatively. "Still," I said, "I've also, at the start of this voyage, spoken words I thought the Fire gave me, but to what harm? Is Robert wrong to seek the wisdom of the Brothers before he acts? Or to obey them as strictly as he can?"

"Do you want to seek out some Sisters when we reach Algiers?"

"Hmm." I sat with that thought as another crate went aloft. "I find that I do," I said finally. "We are all one body, from the first martyrs until today. It might be well for me to remember that, and to seek that fellowship a little more earnestly. Or at least intentionally."

"What if they tell you to stop traveling and submit yourself to a convent?"

I lofted an eyebrow at him. "I will thank them for their wisdom and guidance. And I'll tell them that, as soon as I am able, I will do just that." We chuckled together a moment. I held out my hand for him to grasp. "I don't think I'll mind at all, if we could do that," I murmured.

"Why, Rae-Anna," Thomas replied. "One little storm and you're ready to settle down onto a farm and raise a bunch of little Rae-Annas?"

I smirked. "We'll start with cows. Or goats," I said.

He shuddered. "No goats. Been butted too many times by jealous billies. A milk cow and some chickens, maybe. Wheat and barley for the rest. And I'll have a little Thomas, if you won't have a little Rae-Anna."

"We'll see," I said. I frowned suddenly. "Do you know who never came for confession? Master Kingsley." I twisted around to look at Charlotte; that family appeared to be sleeping. I could only imagine how exhausted they were with fright and anxiety. Mother and daughter, anyway; I envied Jonnie that he had seemed to sleep through much of our journey.

"Probably busy with too many other things," Thomas suggested. "Agnarr's been busy topside, as well."

I hummed. "He would be the closest thing to an actual sailor, among the passengers at least."

"That he is."

"But we also don't know why he's here, do we? Did he ever say?"

He cocked an eyebrow and shook his head. "Maybe we should find out."

We got up and went up the ladder, slipping quickly between groups of passing sailors. On deck, the waves looked much higher than before, and closer together. Every time the bow went down, a heavy spray shot over it and back upon us, the water racing along the deck before pouring either off the side or down a hatch. We were making our way with just the foremast, its sails still small. I glanced back at the Lindwurm; he watched the sailors dumping cargo with as much dispassion as Ginnie had. But after a moment, he looked at me and smiled.

I took a steadying breath, turning around to find Agnarr. He was directly before us, thin hair plastered to his skull, clothes sticking to his skin while the wind flapped a few loose spots like flags. I startled: he looked almost skeletal, and an image of the battle at the convent flashed to mind. *But he said he didn't recognize the language. Did he lie?*

But then he smiled, genuinely pleased to see us, I felt. And my spirit lightened, nearly erasing the iron ball that still rolled occasionally inside me. I returned his smile. "I thought you said we were nearly out of this?" I jibed.

He shrugged, his grin widening. "We are closer now than before."

"Closer to the middle, or the end?" Thomas asked. There was some earnestness to his joke.

Agnarr laughed. "Time will tell. Did the Captain call for hands?" he asked, glancing between us.

"Actually we hoped to talk to you," I said.

He paused to wipe rain from his face. "Jörmungandr is not here for me," he said matter-of-factly.

"I believe you," I said. "But why are you here?"

He glanced briefly aft, then gestured toward the hatch. "I don't mind rain, but I'm also no fish," he said.

I nodded, preceding him quickly back below. I did not mind being out of the rain and the washing decks. Agnarr dripped for a little, then made his way to his hammock. Thomas and I followed. As he neared it, he suddenly took the hem of his shirt and pulled it over his head. The skeletal image was gone, his back a sea of muscles. My eyes goggled before I turned away, blushing. Thomas folded his arms, but kept from frowning.

I heard rummaging, assumed Agnarr was looking for a dry shirt. Finally Thomas touched my elbow and I turned around again. Agnarr was slicking his hair back as he sat on his hammock. He seemed not to notice what he had just done. "I am here," he said instead, his voice pitched just above the storm, "to find a hero."

My brows climbed, and Thomas cleared his throat. "A hero?" he echoed.

Agnarr nodded, his grin flashing. "It has been foretold that when our shackles tighten and our blood is cut off, a hero will be come from the land of the coal-skinned to strike the chains and guide our way."

"What is happening to your people?" I asked.

His grin faded. "We are beset by an ancient terror—some say drachan, some say spirits. They come in the darkness, take sometimes our children, sometimes our animals. No trap has caught it, no fire spooks it away." He shook his head. "We cannot sleep, we are not free to plant our fields or hunt our deer, we cannot forge our steel for trade or war. We are shackled. And each night that it attacks, more of our young are gone. Our blood—the passing down of our blood—is cut off." He drew a sigh, forced his smile back on. "So I come to find our hero."

While he spoke the Fire flickered and warmed, though it brought me no specific guidance. "What is a drachan?" I asked.

His eyes flashed. "A dragon."

I pursed my lips, but at a glance from Thomas held my silence. I would not insult him with a flippant remark about the dragon we had faced. Likely it was not there for the same reason. "How will you know when you find this hero? Do you have a description, or something else from the prophecy?"

"To draw close to this terror, one must come as a sacrifice. To escape again, one must flow like the river as though it grasped at water that seeps through its claws."

I blinked. "That will not be easy to find," I said.

He nodded, pursing his lips. "True. A warrior willing to pretend to be weak, but who holds such strength and..." He swirled his fingers. "I cannot think of the word—able to move exactly and without effort."

"Graceful?" I offered.

He nodded slowly. "Yes. I think you are right. Strength and...graceful? As water moves with strength but flows around our fingers."

"Sounds like The Beloved," Thomas murmured. When I glanced at him, he shrugged. "He went to his passion as a sacrifice, yet escaped the claws of death with power and grace."

"He went as a lamb..." I faltered, swallowing.

Thomas looked quizzically at me. Agnarr's eyes glittered, and he spoke first. "You have an idea of who I seek?"

I bit my lip, but shook my head. Surely not... "I don't think so, but knowing such specifics will certainly help."

He straightened. "You will help me look for this man when we reach Algiers?" he asked.

I took a breath, glanced again at Thomas, felt for the Fire. "Perhaps," I allowed. "Our Father directed us to go with Mahmoud for some reason, it wasn't just to get through this storm. Although..." I trailed off again, looking sideways toward Khalid's hammock. A tongue of Flame rose above the rest. "I think there may be several good works for us to accomplish in Algiers."

Thomas followed my gaze, then grunted. "I think you're right."

I shook myself. "We need to defeat this Lindwurm first. Agnarr, you seem to be on a correct mission—a good work of your own." I paused, considering him anew. "Is that why you are so sure it is not here for you?"

"And my Vala," he replied automatically. "She spoke nothing of my death."

"Yes, that is interesting," I said. I chewed my lip a moment, gazing at Thomas. I would not have expected coinciding prophecies from different sources. And yet, what good would it do Agnarr if she prophesied doom? "Do you fear death?" I asked.

"Only if I were craven," he said solemnly. "As long as I die well, I will see my fathers' halls and drink at their tables."

Robert appeared in the dark, gripping a timber as the boat pitched sideways. He jerked his head toward Agnarr. "You don't run into many of your beliefs," he said. "Not for some hundreds of years, in fact."

Agnarr grinned. "Perhaps *you* do not," he said. "I have heard it since I was a babe in my father's shield."

"Don't do a lot of raiding, though," he pressed.

Agnarr's grin slipped. "I know your fear. It rises like the blood moon. Many are surprised to learn of the *Vik* who stayed in their farmsteads and offered simpler sacrifices. More so to learn that our faith did not die with the final raid." He flashed a smile. "It seems Jörmungandr is real enough."

Robert grunted. "Not according to these two."

I looked up. "You believe he is real?" I asked.

"He seems real enough, there behind us."

"But borne of a faith, as you just pointed out, some centuries beyond its height—among those who worshipped," I said.

"Perhaps he comes now to re-awaken the faith of many grown cold," Agnarr said. He cocked his head. "Your own faith lay dormant for long times as it awaited its savior."

I smiled. It had, but such had been promised. "Why do your gods wait?" I asked.

"To test the faith. See who true believers are."

"Hmm. Mine waited because it was in Our Father's timing. We may not know why until we achieve perfection—I certainly don't know that right now. And yet, the time was what it needed to be. It always is, with Him. Regardless of our faith, or how many or who acknowledge Him—He tends to carry out His plan despite us."

"This is why we are still in Jörmungandr's shadow?" Agnarr asked. "Because it isn't time yet?"

"Fair point; I don't know. I don't think so. I think he remains because we don't know how to battle him yet. That can happen too."

Agnarr's lip curled. "Your god cannot just rid of us him?"

"He could, absolutely. But we would learn nothing. And," I added, striking upon the idea as I spoke it, "perhaps the very reason he does not attack us outright is because Our Father is fighting that part of the battle for us. *But Our Father is faithful, who will not suffer you to be tempted above that ye are able; but will with the temptation also make a way to escape, that ye may be able to bear it.*"

There was some commotion behind us, and we turned swiftly as a group of sailors stood over a crate broken open. They were staring daggers at one another, and a burly one shoved another with an oath.

"What is it?" I asked, quickly rising.

The burly one calmed, nodded his head in deference. "Sorry, miss," he growled. "Accident, is all." He gestured to the others.

I looked down, saw it had been a crate of foodstuffs. "You're throwing food over the side?" I asked.

"That's what I said!" the smaller one said. He was quickly cuffed by the larger.

"Surely Captain Gavril would want us to eat," I offered gently. I made my way to where they stood. "Have you eaten lately?"

"We've been weathering this storm, miss," said the burly one. "Haven't had the time. Or the stomach fer it."

I stooped, picked up a dried apple that was not so dry anymore. I bit into it: it had been cured, still full of flavor if not as crisp. "This is delicious," I said, feeling its nourishment quickly enter me. "Find Mr. Fields, tell him I recommend everyone eat their fill before we throw it over. Rescue is coming soon."

The burly one shoved the smaller one again, then turned to the others. "Keep bringing the rest. And we'll see."

The men scampered off, a new energy suffusing them. My own eyes felt brighter. Rescue was coming. I could feel it.

The ship shuddered as if it struck ground, and I lurched into the large sailor as cries shrieked from above.

Chapter 11

As I righted myself, there was a long groaning scrape that shuddered the ship, then one final thump as it rocked free again. The sailors went up the ladder, Agnarr close behind. The twins had awoken and were crying as Charlotte tried to calm them. I could tell she needed calmed as well. Robert's hands were clasped together as his mouth moved soundlessly.

I sighed, gazing at Thomas. "That was not a mis-interpretation," I said.

"Perhaps our salvation accidentally hit us on the way by to take down the serpent," he said, his mouth quirking in a half-smile.

Thomas went up, but I hesitated. I was no sailor, cured of my seasickness or not. I made my way back toward Charlotte. Ginnie had calmed, but not Jonnie. As I approached, Ginnie's gaze went flat again, and I waited for them to flash red. But she seemed merely disinterested.

This isn't you, is it?

Ginnie's eyes flicked to mine, registered comprehension, then slid aside. She pulled a little away from Charlotte, and I felt a hint of disgust.

"Still an adult?" I murmured as I came alongside their hammock. Ginnie glared, but made no remark. I pitched my voice higher. "Quite an adventure this time, isn't it? I expect your other voyages will pale in comparison with this one, when you recall it."

All three stared at me as though I'd lost my mind, yet I think I had actually found it. "You've never heard the story of how I started, have you?" All three shook their heads. I glanced aside, saw Robert shift his head as though listening, though he stayed in a posture of prayer. "I was at a convent, near a town called Holden. I thought I was cursed because of my left-handedness. Most people did—or still do." I smiled away the bitterness. "I hoped to rid myself of the curse there. But one day blue fire invaded me, would burst from my hand at odd times. And I began hearing a voice that I did not recognize, speaking in ways I don't speak. I thought my curse was worsening, that all the Sisters were in mortal danger. Perhaps Holden as well. They fixed penance upon me, that I undertook with as much strength as I could muster. But it was never enough. By my own means, I could not dispel the fire or be rid of my curse. Finally, the fire caused the death of one of the Sisters, and I waited to be cast out from them, or executed. By then, I wished for it myself.

"Instead, the Sisters comforted me, removed the penance, and tended my hurts and my ignorance of several things. The very moment I thought my doom was finally upon me was the moment that doom broke and fled. There was still a battle to fight—the evil that actually threatened the convent and the town finally revealed itself, and was defeated by the same fire I thought cursed me. In the process, there were many other strongholds broken in my mind that would have kept me from answering Our Father's call on my life when it came at the end. Doctrines that, elevated above my experience of The Beloved rather than held in tandem with it, would have kept me in the convent and not on this journey with Thomas. Despite all the dangers we've faced since, I am in Our Father's hands. And He has promised me that no lives will be lost. So, I'm wondering, what will you walk away from this voyage with? What story will you tell others?"

"Never get on a ship," Jonnie said quietly.

I smiled. "Will you stay in Algiers, then?"

He scrubbed his nose and frowned.

"The serpent will not return, once it is banished," I offered gently.

"It's a beautiful creature," Ginnie murmured.

Charlotte glanced at her, horrified. But I turned my smile to her. "It is, isn't it? In appearance, at least—the glimmering scales, the awesome size of it! I wonder if a redeemed version of it will exist in the New Eden. What do you think?"

"I would like that," Ginnie replied. She sniffled, but kept her gaze cast down. "Will Mister Langford and Mister Adloth come back?"

"I believe they must," I said. I couldn't help flashing a mischievous grin. "I wonder what tales they'll have to tell?"

Charlotte goggled at me. "They seem to be in utter terror!" she squeaked. "Should you speak of it so lightly?"

I lowered my eyes, chastened. "Forgive me," I said. "I have experienced my own terrors, but came out holier for it; perhaps I forget what it was like while I was in them. I pray they find their forgiveness, and whatever path Our Father would lay out for them."

"I do not envy your path," Charlotte said. "Is it always like this for you?"

I pursed my lips. "Yes, and no. In dangers, yes—but always terror?" I shook my head. "Only when I look at the waves, instead of fixing my eyes on The Beloved. When I remember why I am here, what he has ultimately called me to, I would choose none other."

In the dimness, I saw Ginnie's scales fade a little more, retreating from her neck. I held silence though, not wanting to draw attention to it. I felt a nudge that to do so would re-erect some of her walls out of spite, just as they were starting to crumble.

Instead, I patted Jonnie's knee and stood. As I turned, I caught a glimpse of Robert diverting his gaze to return to his prayers. I thought to go over to him next, but saw Thomas crouching on the ladder. When I did, he waved me over and disappeared topside.

As I came up, I saw sailors clustered in knots, scattered across the deck. I glanced at each, then at Thomas' grim smile. It was then, too, I realized the ship was not rocking. I stared around, all the waves still mounting in walls around us, but distantly from the ship.

"What happened?" I asked.

He nodded his head toward the side of the boat, trailing me as I went to the railing. He gripped my arm as I neared. "Careful," he said. I acknowledged him, took shuffling steps nearer. When finally I peered over the railing, I saw the waters almost fifty feet below. I blinked. Leaning over just a little further, I saw the pale gleam from the Lindwurm's scales: he held us aloft by the might of his tail as the winds and rains continued to howl.

I turned and stared at him, and bit back a laugh. I didn't want to taunt him. Yet it seemed so ridiculous to me, such a desperate move to exert what power over us he thought he had. I turned instead to Thomas. "The seas have calmed," I murmured.

He stared wide-eyed. But then a light dawned in his eyes, and I saw his joy return. "Peaceful," he replied.

I looked toward the quarterdeck, saw Gavril with his fists clenched tight behind him as he stared at the Lindwurm. I made my way to him. "Captain," I called as I neared. "Have you had the men eat yet?"

He whirled, staring at me. "Are you a fool?" he spat.

"No, I'm quite empty," I replied, still keeping my voice low. "And I believe your men are as well. We should eat while we can, before casting off the rest of the cargo."

His mouth worked soundlessly. When he glanced at Thomas, something seemed to break. I don't know if he saw the light, or simply gave up. "If you say so," he said. He glanced behind me. "Mr. Fields!" he bellowed. "Have the men eat and gather strength. We'll cast the rest off afterward and pray for land."

I nodded my head toward Gavril, thanking him silently for his faith. He turned away and stalked to his cabin. Perhaps he thought we were going to die either way.

"You heard him!" Fields shouted finally. "Break open those last crates and take food. Be quick!"

Accustomed to obeying orders without questions, the knots of soldiers broke up as they scrambled like ants for the nearest crates of food that poor Langford hoped to re-establish his master's trade with. I glanced at the blue flame where his head floated. Though I saw no recognition in his eyes, his gaze followed the proceedings as if he could see it in some way. Adloth seemed to rest. At least, his eyes were closed, though his mouth twitched time and again in quick frowns.

I hadn't meant to be so casual about it, below with the twins, but I was eager to hear of their experiences wherever they were, and what they were aware of or not. I nearly wished to join them, just to see for myself, but felt no calling toward that.

Thomas brought me some bread and dried fruit, and a piece of smoked meat. "His body," I murmured to Thomas as we broke the bread. We ate, and as I chewed I turned to look again at the Lindwurm. His piercing red eyes bored into me, but his anger washed against me as against a stone quay. *Out of time*, floated across my mind. Salvation was near, it was only a matter of biding. The Lindwurm's time was running short. I looked benignly at the waves. As beautiful as the Lindwurm, only terrible if one feared death by them. *Who shut up the sea with doors, when it brake forth, as if it had issued out of the womb? And brake up for it my decreed place, and set bars and doors, and said, Hitherto shalt thou come, but no further: and here shall thy proud waves be stayed?*

Just as the Lindwurm's smile tightened in a rictus I shouted: "Grab your lines!" I scrambled for the nearest rope and wrapped my wrist around it. Thomas was close behind me, gripping with both of his sinewy farmer's arms as he encircled me. My stomach lurched into my throat as I could tell the Lindwurm's tail retreated and the ship dropped like a stone toward the sea.

My eyes flew wide, the waves so impossibly far away. However well this ship had held up, it could not stand this. *For he commandeth, and raiseth the stormy wind, which lifteth up the waves thereof!*

I prayed it as a reminder of His promise to me, and squeezed my eyes shut. I felt a vibration, a small thud as though the ship settled ungracefully on a wave. I peeked. There was a wall of water behind us; the boat raced down the face of a huge wave that had not been there a moment ago. Twisting, I saw us speeding toward the bottom. The boat pitched, a spray spouted from the bow and hit us like a thousand tiny needles, and the ship was righting itself and slowing as it approached the next wave.

I unclenched my hands as I breathed and the boat returned to its normal storm-tossed rocking. Thomas leaned his head into my neck briefly, and his lips pressed into my sea-soaked flesh. I glanced back:

the Lindwurm seemed disgruntled, but showed no retaliation. *Don't forget who is in charge of the mighty waters.*

His burning gaze fixed me. *My time of waiting is short. The end is coming.*

I kept my thoughts to myself, but I knew he was right. Just, perhaps, not in the way he meant it to sound.

"Who is it?" a shout demanded.

Thomas released me from the railing as we both turned. One of the sailors stared at us in rage. "You said someone sinned, and that's why the serpent is here. Who is it? Bring him out! Is it you?" He took a few stomping steps toward us. "I'll throw you over myself!"

"That won't fix it," I said evenly. "The serpent himself said those two were due him, yet has the storm abated since they went over? Had he shown any concession for their sacrifice?"

"No debtor forgives half a debt," the sailor seethed. "Of course he continues to punish us until the last one is brought to him."

"Are you sure it isn't you?" Thomas asked carefully. The sailor was caught short, his neck throbbing.

"And there is one who forgives our debts—all of our debts, without sacrifice," I went on. "All we must do is turn away from continuing into those debts, and acknowledge them, and He forgives them all. That is how I know this snake is not from Our Father, no matter what he says."

"Well your Father doesn't seem to be here! Where is he?" He spread his hands wide. "That snake plays with us as a cat does a mouse—can your Father not rid us of so much as a cat?"

"Lucky, wasn't it, that that wave appeared from nowhere to catch us. Wouldn't you say, Lennman?" Mr. Fields boomed as he strode across the quarter deck toward us. "I would sooner show gratitude to my worst enemy if he saved me from being stove in by a drop like that."

"I have a family—at home!" he shouted back. And at his own words, something broke in him. His shoulders sagged and every bit of bluster departed as his eyes pleaded with us, with Mr. Fields. "I can't take this storm anymore. I can't take that blasted snake staring at us every moment, knowing our thoughts."

I squinted. "Does he know them?" I asked. "Does he speak to you?"

Lennman's lips thinned, and he frowned. "Of course. We all can hear his taunting." He glanced around, saw mostly blank or wary stares. Only some showed recognition. "Can't we?"

"Aye," came from a few lips.

"Not I," said most of them.

Mr. Fields looked at me. I considered, glancing at Thomas. "Can you spare them, Mr. Fields?" I asked. "I would like to take them below and question them."

He clasped his hands behind his back. "One at a time, anyway," he allowed. "If it'll help us be rid of that thing—"

"I cannot promise this will do it," I interjected.

He nodded. "Well. A chance, then. Start with Lennman. Report to me when you're done," he directed toward the sailor.

I nodded to him, led him to the ladder and down. We stayed further away from Charlotte and the twins, for their sakes and for Lennman's. He stared at them a moment, then crossed himself and slowly turned to Thomas and I.

I could tell something had shifted. "What is it?" I asked.

"That one," he whispered. "She doesn't...I don't think she wants me to speak with you."

I glanced over, saw Ginnie staring at us with her jaw set in a grim line. "Do you fear her?" I asked, turning back.

"I've feared them both since they appeared," he murmured. "But I'll speak, miss."

"What do you hear the serpent saying?"

"Death and all," he replied. "His words are seldom, and often not our tongue. But it's some of his feelings."

"*Senda mér han?*" I asked.

He shook his head slowly. "Not those words, but the accent is the same."

"What feelings, then?"

"Sometimes a chill would come over me, and I'd look back to see him staring at me. Sometimes a heat. Or I'd come to myself all o' sudden-like, off a line. Mr. Fields never caught me, and some of my mates knew well enough, as they'd done the same."

"Nearing the edge? The railing?"

He shook his head again. "The hatch."

I furrowed my brow. "You were coming below?"

He nodded. I glanced at Thomas, who looked equally perplexed. "Maybe abandoning their duties was enough?" I murmured. He shrugged. "Did anyone ever make it down the ladder before coming to themselves?" I asked Lennman.

He started shaking his head again, then held up a finger. "Kelso," he said. He wagged the finger. "Kelso made it down. I thought the Captain had sent him, but he popped back up so fast again I knew what had happened. But none of us ever did anything." He looked at me as if for an answer.

I had none to give. "Do you have any markings on you?"

He glanced down. "A few tattoos, I'll admit." He looked back up regretfully. "We all do foolishness when we're young. Or at sea."

I waved him away. "I'm not so much worried about that. No markings of scales or anything?"

"As the young twin does?" he asked. I nodded, and he shook his head. "Nothing, miss. We wondered that too; far as we know, none of us have anything like it."

I opened my mouth to ask something else when footsteps sounded on the ladder, and another sailor descended. Lennman's head snapped up. "It's still my turn!" he shouted, balling fists.

The young sailor gaped at him. "I was just relieved, Lennman, honest. I was gonna try to rest in my berth a moment…"

Lennman's fists slowly unknotted as his shoulders sagged. "Of course, Perro, of course." He waved him away and turned back to us.

I eased out a breath, studying Thomas.

"Forgive me," Lennman said. "I don't know what… I'm not often so quick to be mad."

"When you came down here, what were you hoping for?" I asked him.

His shoulders heaved once. "I just want that snake gone."

"Why do you think you can hear him, and others cannot?"

"Couldn't guess, miss."

"You said you have a family; do most of the others? Or just those who agreed with you?"

His gaze flickered. "I didn't see all," he said slowly. "But all those who nodded have family, yes."

"Hmm." I offered a smile. "Forgive me for not remembering, but what did you confess to us earlier in this storm? When all the sailors came by my hammock?"

He glanced at Thomas and back. "Same as just now," he said. "I've had it with this sailing all the time. My papa did it, and my grandpapa. I didn't really want it, but it was all I knew. And Papa put his word in with Captain Gavril. I couldn't turn it down, set him off like that—Papa, that is. After this?" He jerked his head sternward.

"I reckon I can take my Papa's ire."

I nodded once. "Very well. We're doing everything we can, all right? For now, please remember the promise: all will make it through alive if we stay on board. *Wait on Our Father: be of good courage, and he shall strengthen thine heart: wait, I say, on Our Father.*"

He bowed his head and nodded it. "I will try, miss. You'll pray for me?"

"We both will—and have," I assured him. "If Mr. Fields can spare Kelso, I would like to speak to him next."

"Thank you, Miss," he said, then hurried topside. I watched Ginnie as we waited. Her eyes stayed glued to the floor. Charlotte seemed to sleep again, and Jonnie with her. Exhaustion from the terrors, I assumed. Charlotte, especially, was so constantly vigilant over her children—I could only imagine the toll it took.

Footsteps sounded again, and I looked up as the sailor descended. There was a rip in his knee, I noticed, not yet patched. I frowned as his face appeared—his hair dripping and plastered over his forehead.

My eyes widened. "Are you Kelso?" I asked.

He nodded, swiping his hair out of his eyes. He was the one who had come down while I was talking to Charlotte and the twins, had revealed to them I was left handed.

The one whose eyes I had thought turned briefly red, as Ginnie's sometimes did.

Chapter 12

"And you can hear the serpent—the Lindwurm? What does he say to you?"

He shrugged, glancing away toward the twins. "Oh, just threats of doom I guess. Not hard to figure out, with this storm the way it is."

"You're not bothered at all by it?" Thomas asked.

"At first, I was. Well, it was strange just to hear him. Beyond what everyone else could hear, the couple times he spoke. But after a while—just like the storm—it gnaws on you so long without killing you, maybe you don't actually have to worry about it."

And yet there was an edge to his voice, to his glances. I thought something worried him. But I didn't want to confront him with that just yet. "Lennman said you were compelled by the serpent, once, that you made it all the way down the hatch where others just came near it."

His gaze went distant, and he blinked. "Oh, right. That. No, I was coming down here to check on something—the hold, to see if more water was coming in. I thought we were riding lower in the waves than at first."

"But as soon as you got down here, you went topside again," I said. "You never checked the hold."

"Right." His eyes flicked furtively toward the twins again.

I frowned, lowering my voice. "Kelso, are you sure that's what you came to check on? Or was something else bothering you?"

He chewed his lip a moment, looked at me and then at Thomas. "Does it matter?"

"It might be very important—if we want to escape this storm. And the Lindwurm."

He rolled his eyes. "You can't call him Jörmungandr? That's his name."

I looked steadily at him. "He's not real, Kelso. Not like you might think."

He rolled his neck, and I caught him again catching the twins out of the corner of his eye. I looked over, saw Ginnie staring at us with great interest. I studied her, then Kelso. "Does she worry you?" I murmured.

"Not her; him," he said. "He's just too...peaceful, for all that's happening to us. And to his sister." He pressed his lips together, glanced angrily at me, then hurried up the ladder again before I could stop him.

I frowned at Thomas. "He's worried about Jonnie?"

Thomas shrugged. "He does kind of have a point. We're so focused on Ginnie because of her changes, but why doesn't Jonnie seem surprised or shocked by it all?"

"He's not unaffected, Thomas."

"But not like the rest. Look at him." He gestured to the trio. "Sleeping again already? I wish I could do that."

I hadn't considered it until then. True, he had screamed or cried in surprise or at the culminations of things, as even hardened sailors had. But most times I looked at him, he was as now: asleep, or resting peacefully in his mother's arms. Was it something about her? "Hmm," I murmured. We made our way aft. Ginnie watched us the whole way, but made no movement or noise. I touched Charlotte's arm, then gently grasped it. She startled awake, her eyes darting to us both as she caught her breath.

"What? What is it? Are the children okay?" She caught sight of Ginnie, who ignored her, then pulled Jonnie closer in her embrace. "Oh. Of course. But what is it?"

"I wanted to wake you first, but I also hoped to wake Jonnie and talk to him for a little bit," I said. "Do you think that would be okay?"

She looked down at him, then again at me. "Do we have to? I'd rather he sleep, if he's comfortable to do so."

"That's what we want to ask him about, actually," I said. When she squinted, I went on. "Is he always so steady? Why doesn't he seem as scared or worried as the rest of us? I would have thought he would be afraid of such a storm."

"It's not his first time sailing," she said, bristling.

I smiled. "Nor did I imagine it was yours."

"Are you sure this is necessary?"

"It may be very important."

"He's not in league with that sea serpent, I can assure you."

Ginnie twisted to stare at her mother. Charlotte tried to hold her gaze, but failed. She kissed the top of Jonnie's head, rubbed his shoulder. "Jonnie dear, wake up. Jonnie?"

Ginnie sulked, then elbowed him hard.

"Ginnie!" Charlotte admonished, as Jonnie grunted himself awake. His eyes cleared, but he kept his peace for a few moments.

"It's still storming," he said. He looked at me. "We're not in port yet?"

I shook my head. "I'm afraid not." I smiled at him. "I must admit, Jonnie, I'm envious of you. You're taking this adventure quite well. Aside from a few brief moments of doubt."

"Well, you said we'd make it through, didn't you? I guess I just wanted to sleep until we got there."

I braved a glance at Charlotte. "Not everyone believes me like you do. They see the serpent, see a captain who can only do his best…"

"Oh, no," Jonnie shook his head vigorously. "That's all the more reason. He's not just any captain—he's my dad."

Charlotte's mouth set a grim line when I sharpened my gaze on her. "I didn't know that," I said.

Charlotte nodded. "It's not really fair to the sailors. They can't take their families aboard. So we don't make it obvious, or show favorites. We sleep in normal passenger berths if we ever sail with him."

"He *is* the captain," I said with a shrug. "And it's his—and your father's—boat."

"He's very particular about it, though," she said. "Sometimes tries to act like we aren't even his family."

"So I noticed," I said drily. "He shows great restraint, given these are his children," I added, trying not to look too obviously at Ginnie.

Ginnie just folded her arms and sank lower. Charlotte smiled and nodded. "It can be hard. But then, it's hard on everyone."

"Ginnie," I said, turning directly to her now. "How do you feel about your brother? Do you love him?"

"Well, I can't hate him—what is there to hate?" she scoffed. "May as well hate a wet carpet."

"Ginnie!" Charlotte cried again, this time giving her a light backhand on her shoulder.

"He's an infant. He's harmless, guileless, aspirationless, sinless—useless!" She huffed, poking his side.

He only flinched, turned his face toward her. "I love you too, sis," he said. He turned his gaze back to me. "She does love me, she's just afraid to admit it. She's too busy trying to fit me into her personality."

"Is what she said about you true, then? Maybe except for being useless."

"Oh, I'm useless to her. I try to be harmless. No one is sinless, right?" I nodded. "That's what I thought Papa said. And what are aspirations?"

Ginnie shook her head in frustration as I hid a smile. "When you want to be someone or do something significant."

"Oh. Well I'm sure I will be, but I don't know what I would do about it now. I'm just a child."

Ginnie held her hand, palm up, as if to say *Do you see?* But what I saw was a lightening even further of the scales on her arm and hand. Whatever grip the serpent had on her was all but gone. "Will you be a captain, like your father?"

He shrugged. "We'll see. I like sailing. But I like when mama reads stories to me, too. Maybe I'll be a storyteller."

I nodded. "You'll have an interesting one to tell, after this."

He smiled, closed his eyes, and I thought perhaps went straight back to sleep. I shook my head and marveled. "Thank you, both of you," I said. Charlotte only nodded, her eyes darting furtively to Ginnie. I rose, and Thomas and I went back to our hammocks. I lay back, my thoughts racing.

"Well, if Jörmungandr's intent is to breed fear in the chaos, I could see him feeling threatened by that one," Thomas said.

I nodded absently, picking at my lip. Jonnie's approach was interesting, to say the least. And I couldn't fault him for it—it felt proper, in its way. And yet there were many who followed The Beloved with far more vigor and determination. Perhaps His call on them was more urgent. But I couldn't tell.

"Do you think life in Our Father's Kingdom is like a path, or a garden?" I asked Thomas.

"Well, I like gardens," he said.

I smiled at him. "Of course you do."

"How do you mean, then?" he asked.

"Well, if it's a path, then we just need to take the next right step. No matter what comes, just keep moving forward, don't stray off the path, and everything He has intended for us will come along eventually. If it's not changing yet, it's because it isn't supposed to change yet."

Thomas nodded slowly. "I can see that. Faith to hold on, to trust Him—*Strait is the gate, and narrow is the way, which leadeth unto life, and few there be that find it.* But also Saint Paul's admonition: *I have learned, in whatsoever state I am, therewith to be content.* Why 'content' except you have what you should?"

"All of that," I replied, still smiling. He was such a blessed partner to have. "A garden, though, allows you to move around. Still with borders, that you must stay inside of. But other than that, you may grow what you want, eat of its fruit when it matures, tend it as Our Father gives you wisdom. If there's something you want but do not have, you go and get it. Unless it lies outside the garden."

He frowned. "Interesting. And there is, of course, Eden to look to. *And Our Father commanded the man, saying, Of every tree of the garden thou mayest freely eat.*"

"And from the Preacher: *Whatsoever thy hand findeth to do, do it with thy might.* And again from Saint Paul: *Whether therefore ye eat, or drink, or whatsoever ye do, do all to the glory of Our Father.* Maybe we're not talking about eating and drinking specifically, but he said 'whatsoever you do.'" I paused as he nodded agreement. "But here's the problem: if His Kingdom is a garden, and we live as though it were a path, we may deny ourselves things, keep ourselves from accomplishing His work because we're waiting for it to come to us, when He expects us to go and get it. But if it is a path, and we live as though it were a garden, we risk straying from the narrow, believing we're only chasing a godly desire. And perhaps we've been fooled by an angel of light."

Thomas was silent for a time, and I supposed he was considering this quandary I'd presented him. But after several long moments I realized his eyes were unmoving, instead of wandering like when he was thinking. But he stared at me, as though he thought I already knew the answer. "I'm asking you seriously," I said.

He drew a short breath. "Rae-Anna," he said slowly. "Why are you asking...me?" I blinked, not sure what he meant. Another breath. "Why aren't you asking Our Father? You speak as though you don't have a relationship with Him. I mean, you may as well ask Robert if being my wife is like walking a path or growing a garden."

I swallowed, knowing I was fighting tears but not wanting that to show. "What is life as your wife like?" I asked instead. "Do you have a narrow road for me, or a garden?"

"You want to know if you can just command the storm to stop, and the serpent to leave," he said.

My heart sank a little. I did want to know that, but his tone ridiculed the idea. *"And all things, whatsoever ye shall ask in prayer, believing, ye shall receive,"* I said.

"The essence of asking is the possibility of being denied," he responded.

I grinned weakly. *"Thou shalt tread upon the lion and adder: the young lion and the dragon shalt thou trample under feet."*

He cocked an eyebrow. "Haven't you? I mean, in a way. You've said over and over, any true sea serpent of that size would just drag us under and be done. Maybe Our Father consented to your first command over the smaller serpent not to harm Ginnie."

"Or He is staying faithful to His word from the beginning," I said. "We both heard that promise, and others as well. So what's the point of those other scriptures?"

Thomas rubbed his knees. "Well, taking it logically from a point where we think we can just send off whatever threatens us, couldn't we just command all evil to leave the world, and usher in paradise right now?"

I considered him. "We can only protect our own souls," I said slowly. "And the serpent isn't here for us."

Again he stared blankly at me. "I thought you already knew that."

I smiled chidingly. "Knowing it, and believing it despite all, are two different things."

He frowned. "Despite what all?"

"Getting everything wrong," I said, losing my voice in a whisper.

"Getting what wrong?" he asked, growing bewildered.

I sighed. "Probably everything. From the start, maybe even—well, okay, the Fire is safe. Your Seed is safe. But what are we doing out here, all alone? Throwing ourselves into situations we know nothing about, so convinced we have all the answers and we cast them like bread in the Coliseum as people—real, living souls—fight and die to the cheers. What right do we have? What special knowledge do we think we have that we think we can counsel others? We've been faithful for, what, less than a year? Married for a few months? And we think to command this ship as if we know!" I finally stopped to take a breath as Thomas held up his hands.

"What happened that you question this, so suddenly?" he asked.

"I've been afraid of this for a long—"

"No, something happened on this ship."

I huffed, looking toward the hatch. I could see—or thought I could—the blue flickering of Langford's torch. And Adloth's. Around the opening the light danced, mocking the blue fire that had entered me in the convent. *I do not question you,* I repeated to myself. I was done with questioning the Flame. But the idea that evil would so blatantly use an appearance of the Sacred Fire, twist it so horrendously to lead so many astray, made me sick.

I frowned. It wasn't Adloth, it was before that. That seed of doubt germinated before anyone had gone overboard. No, it sprouted when I became sick. *When had I become sick?*

"When I brought up Jonah," I said. My eyes flicked to Thomas as he blurred through my tears. "I was sure of the word spoken over this boat and crew, until I mentioned Jonah."

"That didn't come from the Fire," Thomas said. "That came from you."

I nodded miserably. "I was trying to prove..." I trailed off as what I saying struck me. "I was trying to prove I was right," I finished, swallowing.

"To who? Yourself?"

"Partially. But also to Robert."

Thomas nodded once. "Ah. I wondered." He drew a breath. "How Our Father works through him is probably different than for us, you know. From what we learned, what he was when he was called is far different."

"So you think he's right to only seek the Brothers? And obey them?"

Thomas shrugged. "Maybe he has to—maybe his faith, right now, only permits him that. It's possible, you know, that if he tried to follow his own ideas—well, not ideas, but you know what I mean. Maybe he would go astray. So, for now, he seeks outside wisdom and is obedient to it. That's not a bad thing, is it?"

"As long as it's not a bad thing for us to step out on our own, as we perceive the Sacred Fire prompting us."

He smiled gently. "I think what we've learned so far is that it's only bad if we step outside the prompting of the Fire."

I took his rebuke in its intent. "We can say that for sure." I drew a cleansing breath. "So, what next?"

He sat for a moment, then closed his eyes. I let myself drift down into the Fire, found comfort in its warmth. The movement of the ship became something other, something that rotated around us. The storm raged, but outside. I felt nourishment, as well, from the refuge, a strong castle well-stocked against siege. Security, comfort, and sustenance all in one. *Forgive me for denying Your refuge, for running from the peace You provide. We still seek your wisdom, though...*

And he joined himself with him to make ships. Then Eliezer prophesied, saying, Because thou hast joined thyself with Ahaziah, the LORD hath broken thy works. And the ships were broken, that they were not able to go.

I looked at Thomas the moment his eyes snapped open. "You know who we never talked to," he said.

I smiled grimly. "Master Kingsley," I said.

I caught a flash of red in my periphery, heard Ginnie's sibilant phrase repeated again, and my stomach went cold. I spared her one glance, caught fear in the eyes of a little girl now fighting against that which tried to possess her. Thomas led the way topside. As soon as we came up, Agnarr was before us, face ghostly white.

"Where's Master Kingsley?" I asked him.

His lip trembled. *"Er ist im Feuer."*

I stared at him, confused. Thomas touched my sleeve, and I knew he pointed. But I kept my gaze on Agnarr. "That's not from the Northern people," I said.

He blinked, taken aback. "You speak their words now?" he asked.

I snorted. "No, but I've heard every word for 'fire' in that language, and you didn't use one of them. You are not the Vik reborn, are you?"

He smiled sadly. "It is a long story."

"All of us have long stories," I said wearily. "And some of us aren't living the ones we should." I cut myself off abruptly and shook my head. "Actually, none of us are—are we?"

I glanced at Thomas, who studied me. It was time to have the Captain gather everyone left alive on deck, and face this serpent—this Jörmungandr, who was supposed to be a Lindwurm.

Chapter 13

Boots rang across the deck as Mr. Fields and Captain Gavril approached. I wiped wet hair from my forehead and watched them come. They seemed...apprehensively hopeful? I had not helped their mood by sending a sailor to get them with ambiguous words. In my defense, I was not absolutely sure this would work. So many of my ideas had fallen short up to now.

"Have you discovered—" Gavril stopped, staring at Kingsley's disembodied head freshly in the blue fire. He lowered his eyes in shame. "I didn't know he was so near his end," he murmured.

"Your father-in-law?" I asked.

He glanced up sharply, dark eyes glittering. "Did Charlotte tell you that?"

"She confirmed it, once Jonnie told us the source of his peace. His father was the captain," I said. "He trusts you completely to get us through this storm unscathed."

His jaw clenched. "Faith of a child," he said.

I nodded with a cocked eyebrow. "As all followers of Our Father are supposed to," I said. "His word alone should define our reality, not anything else we see, hear, or feel. Not even—" I nodded toward the stern. "Storms or serpents."

"It is lack of faith that keeps it near?" he asked.

I smiled. "In a manner of speaking. But I need every sailor and passenger here on the deck. In Fosse, there were attitudes shared by the entire castle that brought a dragon, and only by addressing them all could we reduce the wyrm small enough to defeat. I may need to do the same here."

"Of course. Mr. Fields, make it so." As the first mate went off with bellows and whistles, Gavril turned to me. "Any particular place on deck?"

"Where they can all hear me."

He smiled wryly. "I'm afraid, Miss Rae-Anna, with this storm there is nowhere but directly beside you that they can all hear you."

I let out a short sigh. "And if there was no storm? Where could they hear me then?"

He cocked his head toward the quarter deck and, at my gesture, led me up to it. I stood at the rail in front of the helmsman as sailors were starting to gather by ones and twos below. *So much like Fosse,* I thought.

Remember ye not the former things, neither consider the things of old.

I grinned to myself: speak only the words I was about to be given, then. There was still the matter of the storm, though. I bowed my head, sank into the Fire as I prayed. *How then shall they call on him in whom they have not believed? and how shall they believe in him of whom they have not heard? and how shall they hear...*

Unless this storm calms so that my voice may carry?

I looked up, feeling my stomach steady as fresh air filled my lungs. The rain abated, the wind slacked. As before, the waves moved far off. We were still surrounded, but our boat only eased gently back and forth. And we were not a hundred feet in the air. I did not glance back at the Lindwurm. His presence or absence made no difference.

The sailors stood frozen, nervous eyes darting to the calm. Eventually, they all turned to me. Thomas stood nearby, offered me a smile when I glanced his way. I needed to find some way to make my love for him known, for just such moments as these.

"This has been some storm," I said to those gathered. "When we arrive in Algiers, and wherever you go after that, you will carry this story forever. There will be many who won't believe you, will think it the raving of delirious sailors too long at sea. But each of us—" I glanced into many eyes, letting them feel the weight— "Each of us will know what really happened. And each of us, hopefully, will be changed for the better because of it."

"It would be nice to see some land, lass," someone growled. A few nodded agreement. Many folded their arms tightly.

I chuckled. "Do you think we near the edge of the world? And here I thought we were only in the middle of it." A few joined me with smiles. Others swallowed, still nervous. "Our Father told me a story while we were still ashore. Most of you know it. A story foretold of dangers, some loss, but ultimately: safe passage for all on board. Our Father is very interested in stories, did you know that? Most of His Holy Words are stories. Very human stories of our inability to be faithful, and His inability to be unfaithful."

A few folded arms dropped, and I nodded at their unspoken acknowledgement. "Time and again, Our Father held back promised destruction. *Our Father is not slack concerning his promise, as some men count slackness; but is longsuffering to us-ward, not willing that any should perish, but that all should come to repentance.* All of us! He waits, calling to us all '*How often would I have gathered thy children together, even as a hen gathereth her chickens under her wings.'* Amid this storm, this endless torrent of rain, and wind, pursued by imminent death, He would yet save us."

"Then why doesn't he?"

I gazed a long moment at the speaker as the wind shrieked in agreement. When it died down, I spoke: *"Ye would not!"* I took in their astonished gazes, knowing they each thought they would be free if they could. But this is what I was sent to tell them. "Our Father is very concerned with stories," I repeated. "But not so much with the story we wish we could tell, but what story He wants to tell through us."

"A story of calm waters would be nice, right about now," a sailor growled.

I fixed him with my gaze. "Do you trust Captain Gavril?" I asked. "Do you trust him to continue to keep this ship together until we pass through this storm?"

"He's only human," the same man retorted.

I chuckled. "Is he? To his son, he is nearly a god. According to Jonnie, we'll make it through alive simply because his father is the Captain. No other reason. But that's not entirely what I'm asking. So far, I've heard from none of you the thought of throwing Gavril overboard and instating Mr. Fields as Captain, or some other."

"He's a good captain, our captain," someone else piped up. "He's taken us through plenty before."

I saw lights beginning to dawn. "He has taken you through storms before," I reiterated. "Would you trust me to guide this ship? Of course not: I've never been on the water at all, let alone during trying times. Difficult times come to us all. To navigate them, we first need to trust the One who promised to carry us through. Then we need to take what we have learned and help others through, as well."

I shook my head. "No story of a life of ease and comfort will aid anyone, except those similarly-born. But we who would follow The Beloved must *go out into the highways and hedges, and compel them to come in, that His house may be filled.* I can promise you those who live on the outskirts care not how easy you have it, but how you have persevered in the face of adversity. They need to hear of faithfulness, not ease—unless you can promise a world free from troubles."

A few, I could tell, were sorting through my words as they looked inwardly toward The Beloved. Many, I could also tell, still suffered from warring desires. I pressed on. "You want peace. I understand, believe me. And The Beloved is the Prince of Peace—He desires peace for our souls, no matter our outward circumstances. Is that not true strength of being? Not that the seas are calm, but that we are calm despite the turbulent seas. I was amazed by Jonnie, in disbelief that he slept so much despite the howling winds and driving rains. And when I woke him? He observed, quite calmly, that we were not yet at port." I shook my head in chagrin as I thought of it. "The promise was given to many of us—but only one believed it so thoroughly as to assume it. Jonnie rested, waiting for us to arrive as we had been promised. He heard what our story was to be, and waits in utter peace for it to be fulfilled.

"How many of you are peacefully living out the story you were told to live?" I asked suddenly. Most stared. A few shifted uncomfortably. "How many were given a dream, a direction, a purpose, perhaps even long ago, and you have spent the days since doing what was good, and waiting for it to be fulfilled?" I smiled ruefully. "I know I haven't. I've told you my story, how it originated in the convent. And yet I have questioned and worried and doubted that call ever since. Is it truly the Sacred Fire of Our Father? Will He protect and guide me? Can He heal my deepest wounds—not the scars of my face, but the scars on my soul and spirit?" I paused again to look at each in turn. "Did He actually call me to this, or should I listen to another? Who am *I* to truly hear Him?"

Robert began to bluster, and I spread my palms in a calming motion. "That is not *my* story," I emphasized. "I went astray thinking my story must match others also called by The Beloved. But why give us The Body if we are all separate members? If we all are to seek Him alone, why meet together? Why would we have prophets and apostles and teachers if we all are to gain wisdom through Him alone, by our own private and careful worship? He has promised *me* to be my light and guide when I am alone—because I was abandoned in the Convent even surrounded by those who should have helped. Those who would have helped, if the wearing of time had not eroded their compassion and their sensitivity to the work of Our Father. They, too, sought to live a different story than what they had committed to, what Our Father had written for them, because the story they began to weave became comfortable." I chuckled, thinking back on it. "They, too, were not persuaded at first, *though one rose from the dead.* For them, it took many rising from the dead to wake them from their stupor."

I felt a shuddering, knew the serpent began to writhe. He would not delay much longer. "And so I sought to prove myself, to prove that what Our Father gave to me was true. I spoke words He had not given me, but I *have seen vanity and lying divination, saying, Our Father saith: and Our Father hath not sent them: and they have made others to hope that they would confirm the word.* You all saw the fruits of that, and thought I was in league with the serpent. *Therefore thus saith Our Father; Because ye have spoken vanity, and seen lies, therefore, behold, I am against you, saith Our Father.*" I paused, my lip trembling, but soon pressed on as a spout of water shot up near the stern. "*And mine hand shall be upon the prophets that see vanity, and that divine lies: they shall not be in the assembly of my people, neither shall they be written in the writing of the house of my Chosen. And ye shall know that I am The Father."*

I drew a deep breath. "I abandoned the story The Beloved was writing through me, and sought another. Each of us, for one reason or another, have left the stories being written for us, to try to write our own. Adloth was a performer, a tumbler with a troupe. A very good one, who felt hindered by the troupe he was with. He hoped, by leaving them, he might achieve grander heights. But it should not have been. I don't know what story he might have told if he had stayed, but it would not be one wreathed in blue flame," I finished, gesturing to the torch that bore his head. "Langford, too, strove for more than his allotment. Dissatisfied with his lower position he fabricated a higher one. Without the support of the truth, it quickly collapsed. Now he fears his story is over, and does not even seek another. He would do worse than rewrite his story, but bring about its unnecessary conclusion. That, I can promise you, had no part of Our Father's story for us. He wrote the beginning; it is only by His permission that the end should be written.

"Then there was Master Kingsley. I cannot say for certain—perhaps Captain Gavril or Charlotte can give us insight. But my inclination is that this boat was not supposed to be built."

Gavril drew breath sharply, and I smiled grimly as I turned my gaze to him. "Have I hit the mark, Captain?"

He sighed and nodded. "You have, Lady, though I know not how. It had been meant to be for passengers alone. He felt a desire to build something to carry people between lands. He thought, perhaps, the Holy Words might spread further if those called to distribute it had more affordable means to travel. But halfway into the building, he worried about affording it. So we built the rest to carry shipping."

"And why the sailors must carry crates through a hatch, instead of lifting it directly from the hold," I said. He nodded, and I saw a few of the sailors smile thinly. They had put up with it, trusting the Captain and builder in vain. "Master Kingsley despaired now, wondering if he had built the boat the way he was supposed to, much of this would not have occurred." I glanced across the gathered sailors and passengers. "I do not think that is why," I said. A few seemed unperturbed. Some relieved. Others looked quizzically at me. I smiled. "For one thing, the storm has not yet stopped, and we are not suddenly in Algiers. But, more so, there is one yet we have not addressed. Agnarr," I continued, gazing at him. "You named him Jörmungandr, named his attributes, told us all what we should expect from him. And yet assured us you would gain no harm from him."

He gaped a moment. "I do not control him!" he blurted.

I cocked an eyebrow. "No, but he is most after you, who would call on the gods of the Vik. You who have no part of that people—for you are not of the North, but the tribes of the Diutisch." He frowned stubbornly, and so I continued. "When you first saw the serpent, you fell back on the myths of your people, calling it 'Lindwurm,' a land-based creature you admitted to seeing. Then, when Ginnie and the serpent spoke in the language of the north, you could not understand it. 'Send him to me!' she said over and over, marking for the serpent's belly those who would soon cast themselves overboard. And, if I am not mistaken, when you saw Master Kingsley in the flames you uttered your mother tongue in your shock and dismay."

"The child never said that of me," he said, nearly desperate.

"No, for if she did we might all be free. You see, The Liar is also interested in stories—stories where all people are stolen and oppressed. Either they reject Our Father, stolen away by his lies. Or do no work for Him, and His Kingdom does not advance, oppressed as we are by trying to live as others would have us, rather than what Our Father has called us to. Saint Petrif feared sinking, when The Beloved had called him to walk on water. All the apostles feared the loss of their ship, when He had called them to cross to the other side. The Last Apostle knew those on board would be saved, though the ship would be lost, and found hope and providence in that knowledge. That is the promise we have been given."

"Then why did you speak to us of Jonah?" another sailor, nearer the blue torches, demanded.

"I admitted, in part, to my own pride in that," I said. "And yet, I was given Jonah as a sign. And I wondered why. Jonah was the warning," I shouted, as the Lindwurm began to shriek. I had mere moments to convince them. "Jonah knew his story was to be one of the salvation of the Ninevites. And he wanted no part. Imagine: he had heard the stories of prophets who declared death and destruction against evil, and saw those promises fulfilled. And he wished desperately for that story to be told through him! But even in his desperation, he knew that if he obeyed, Our Father's mercy would be shed upon those who hated and cruelly oppressed his people. When he could not get away, he relented and obeyed, still hoping for a story of destruction. And when it did not happen he grew angry once again, until Our Father chided him for his hypocrisy. For prophecy always comes not just to promise judgement but to provide an opportunity for repentance! Now, Agnarr, is your opportunity," I said, turning again to him. "*If we confess our sins, he is faithful and just to forgive us our sins, and to cleanse us from all unrighteousness.*" I held up a finger in warning as he opened his mouth. "*If we say that we have not sinned, we make him a liar, and his word is not in us.*"

His mouth snapped shut, and he began to tremble. I thought perhaps, in someone more emotional, it might turn to weeping. But he held it in, squashed it deep if he could. The trembling began where his sorrow threatened to break out.

"You were sent to save your people," I pressed. "But not by finding some hero far away." I observed the set of his jaw and felt a light creeping in. "Or perhaps you were. Because such a hero could not be found where you came from—rather, could not be forged in your village. He had to be made somewhere else and brought back. You thought it would be someone else you would find in some distant land. But that hero—" I pointed at him— "is to be you."

The trembling stopped and a light sparked in his eyes, growing in brightness and intensity as the Lindwurm bugled. Waves again struck the boat and I grasped frantically at the railing. Sailors spilled everywhere as the boat hewed, some sliding to the railing before they found handholds.

The truth was out. Now the serpent would spend its last desperate attempt to destroy us before that truth could have its effect.

Chapter 14

Much of my memory of that battle was rain, thunder, shouting, and scrambling. The ship bucked upon the seas and upon the serpent's rolling coils, pitching in unnatural ways—bow up, portside down; portside up, stern down. No wave made by wind and Our Father would have sent that ship reeling the way it did.

Sailors scrambled, sometimes on their own wisdom, to lash down things breaking free or to throw things over that could not be lashed down. The sails whipped and tore free, rigging groaned, timbers creaked. Somehow none of them tore or shattered.

I tried mostly to stay out of the way, but would not go below, no matter Thomas' protests. The battle was up here, and despite the truth setting some sailors free, the size of the Lindwurm had not reduced one iota. His massive head loomed over, jaws agape, drool hitting the deck and sizzling. Anywhere it struck, a tiny blue flame sprouted. The wind and rain did not put them out, and stamping on them only pricked the foot of the stomper. Wet canvas had no effect either. And so we let the spots burn as we sought only to hold the ship together, and to keep ourselves on board.

Thomas and a few of the others wielded swords, now, leaning out to pierce the coils as they struck against the sides of the boat. The Lindwurm would shriek, perhaps a tiny bloom of red spotted its side, and a new coil would arise unblemished. It was simply too large, and I began to sense that the sea would heal it too quickly for us to defeat it that way. But, for their part, they reduced some of the battering the poor ship received.

Gavril was shouting again, and I saw a group of sailors running forward with ropes. They tossed them over the prow, and as they drifted back, drew them tight around the ship.

"What's happening?" I shouted, drawing near to the captain.

"Seams are bursting below," he replied. "We're trying to make her fast, but she won't take much more of this. We need to be free of the serpent at least, even if not the waves. He's going to stove us in."

I turned and glared at the serpent, who only leered at me with an evil grin as another coil slammed into the ship. I looked across the deck, saw Agnarr heaving on a line, drawing it tight. I made my way across, dancing through the spots of flames and catching my balance as the ship whirled. I misstepped once, and fire lanced through my foot. I stomped again.

You are a manifestation of evil only—thrice powerless, for our King has defeated you, you have no physical presence in this world, and you are not part of this story. No serpent beset the Last Apostle at sea!

Still that insufferable grin leered down, and more saliva dripped to blue fire. I snorted at the beast, then finally reached Agnarr. I gripped his shoulder and he turned. "Tell me again what evil besets your village," I said.

He only glowered, then moved to another line.

"It's here because of you!" I said, pursuing him. "Whatever Our

Father would have you do, you must accept it."

"I will be free!" he shouted, whirling on me. "I will choose. I will not be oppressed. It is my life."

"Tell me about your life," I said. "Where did you grow up?"

He growled, turned back to his work. I moved beside him, assisted as I could. We worked together for a time, sidestepping fires and securing the ship. I did little more than hold things steady, or hand him things; it was his back and the strength of his arms that were of real effect. "I grew up mostly on farmland," I said. "Holden is not large, and it's a short step from the streets to the fields. I would spend evenings looking out over the rolling hills, grains waving like the sea—calmer seas than this, though," I added with a wry grin. "Flocks were on the hillsides. Sometimes when the sun was low, I would watch the shepherds bringing in their herds, their long shadows stretching across the vale in golden light."

"I grew up in the deep forest," he said. "My ancestors had cleared a small glen. Not much pasture, but we had some cows. Most of our sustenance came from the forests and trees." He pressed his lips together as he hauled on another line. He flinched and ducked as spittle dripped nearby.

"Where did you find peace?" I asked.

He ignored me for a time, bending to his work. I handed him a loose end, and he sighed and swiped water from his face. "The Himmelbuhrt," he said finally. I squinted. "It was a fir, the tallest in our territory, said to touch the sky. In the morning the winds blew soft, and stirred the pines. We celebrated solstices there, especially winter. The gods touched it, I was taught, and by sacred interaction we could be touched by the gods as well."

There was something in his tone, a finality, a deep hurt. I felt the Fire tugging toward it. "What happened to it?" I asked.

He lashed the rope tight, yanking the knot. He looked at me with more than rainwater in his eyes. "Followers of your Beloved cut it down, claimed it led my people astray. Told us all that we could see or sense was evil. Commanded us not to worship wood and stone but something we had never heard of before, had no place in our village or our people." He gazed at me for a long moment, unflinching this time as the massive maw of the Lindwurm passed overhead with another shriek. "You claim the same gods, but found peace in what you could see?"

I drew a breath. "Everything we see and sense has been twisted by The Liar," I said. "And yet *the heavens declare the glory of Our Father; and the firmament sheweth his handywork. Day unto day uttereth speech, and night unto night sheweth knowledge. There is no speech nor language, where their voice is not heard. Their line is gone out through all the earth, and their words to the end of the world.*"

"Then why did they cut down the Himmelbuhrt?"

"Not everyone who claims knowledge possesses it perfectly," I said. "Perhaps they thought, as the drunkard must abhor ale to remain sober, so the only way out from under your gods was complete banishment of all your objects of worship. But I am not certain that decision must be made for you by others."

The ship lurched; he caught himself easily, I stumbled and fell backward. I screamed, scrabbling for the deck as I slid across it on a sluice of water. He started for me, but other hands grabbed me and my head struck only lightly against the rail. I looked up at Thomas, whose eyes were on the Lindwurm as it passed overhead. With a mighty splash his head plunged into the water. His body spun overtop of us like a free rope, scales glimmering as water spattered the deck. Another splash and his head soared up from the opposite side of the deck, circling again.

"He's going to squeeze us asunder," Thomas breathed. As if in confirmation, the first coil snapped tight across the deck as the second formed loosely. The glowing eyes of the snake tracked us as it went down the other side of the ship, looping and looping itself around us.

Thomas leapt forward, sword stabbing downward. But where he had once been able to prick the beast, the sword now bent under his blow without appearing to harm the Lindwurm a scratch. Thomas grunted as the hilt sprang backward, catching him alongside his head. His legs loosened, yet somehow he kept his feet.

Agnarr came to me and helped me to my feet, then rushed to Thomas. He drew his own two-hander, bringing a crashing blow along the scales. It had as little effect, and as the serpent coiled over once more, I saw the blue-flame torches below him. He paused there, eyeing the souls trapped inside. I ducked below his body, sliding on hands and knees across the slick deck. I finally came up near Kingsley. All three stared upward as though they could see the Lindwurm's body overhead.

His maw opened, and water cascaded down. The torches sputtered, the visages of the men inside tattering and ripping as the flames nearly went out. Their voiceless cries renewed as though their bodies were being torn apart in reality. The Lindwurm went below again, then came up with water dripping in overflow from his mouth. In horror I knew one more deluge might actually extinguish the souls of those men.

I rushed forward, burying my hands in each torch as the Fire inside me roared. The blue flames sprang up anew, twice their height, and more of the bodies of the men showed. They were not heads only! That was simply all the fire could show!

Water poured over me, drenching me with liquid fire. I gritted my teeth, knowing my own Fire was a refuge against the assault. But still it hurt. With a tenacious moan I clung to the torches, the Lindwurm's tainted waters running off me in the refreshing rains of the storm. Once again I gripped the torches, placed my palms in their baskets, and prayed for the souls of Kingsley, Langford, and Adloth.

Their flames roared even higher, joining the roar of the Lindwurm, who saw his efforts thwarted. As the blue flames licked against the serpent's scales, Kinglsey rose to his full height and stepped from the fire onto the deck. He staggered and fell as one pulled from icy waters, heaving and sobbing. Langford came next, eyes wide and rolling, though praise and thanksgiving poured from his mouth. Adloth, after agonizing moments, fell over in the fire and crashed to the deck, senseless.

Now the Lindwurm roared his anger anew, passing over the ship again, dripping his fiery spittle and scattering flames like coals across the deck. I ran to the three castaways, checking their state and reassuring them as I could. Soon enough sailors came over, helping Kingsley and Langford to their feet and hurrying them to safer parts of the deck. Adloth remained as one unconscious, and though I shook him, prayed for him, sheltered him from the body and fires of the Lindwurm, he lay still on the deck.

A final coil of the serpent ringed the ship and pulled tight. Agnarr came to me, sword still in his hands. "You must come back," he said. "If you are caught in his coils when the ship breaks—"

"He is not real, Agnarr!" I shouted. I glared at him as he took a step backward. "Fine; so misguided followers cut down your tree. What attached you to the Vik?"

He glowered. "The Vik wreaked much havoc against the followers, in their time," he said. "Their gods could defeat yours once; I wanted them to defeat him again."

I shook my head. "Agnarr, you did not seem so hateful this whole trip. You did not care that I was a follower before. What changed?"

"I still do not care that you are a follower," he said quietly. He snorted a chuckle. "When I saw how you took to a boat, I knew you were no threat. Nor your husband. You would not come after me to convert me, or cut me off from my gods."

I drew a breath. "That time has ended, Agnarr. Perhaps your Vala was right, and you will not fall to the Lindwurm. But the rest of us will die if you don't send him away. This is the story you would live—not just the gods, but the enemies of your gods as well. And right now, those enemies are winning. Don't worry about whether your god can defeat mine, but whether he can defeat the serpent."

Agnarr's eyes darted around, but his lips were pressed in a grim line. "I don't... The power is not mine..." His gaze found me and bored in. "This is not what I would choose."

"You have two choices," I said. *"For they that are after the flesh do mind the things of the flesh; but they that are after the Spirit the things of the Spirit.* You can choose to follow Our Father, and live in what He created you to be; or you can follow your own desires and live in death."

He grit his teeth. "Says you."

I shrugged. "So, I would guess, says the Himmelburht."

He blinked, confused. "What? Are you saying it chose to be cut down?"

"Of course not!" I retorted. He relaxed a moment. "Nor did it choose to be an object or a center of your worship, did it?"

"It..." He hissed, ducking aside as more blue fire rained from the Lindwurm. "We adored it because it grew tall and touched the faces of the gods!"

"It did not. But the point is it grew into the tall tree it was supposed to. It did not try to be a bush or a thistle. If you were drawn to it, it was because it became a pinnacle of what it was created to be. You, if you want to mold your life after the Himmelburht, you must start by declaring who you actually are, not what you wish to be out of vengeance."

The ship groaned, and timbers cracked with loud booms. Sailors cried out, and some made for the rail as though to jump overboard. But Paul's story rang in my ears and I shouted: "You must stay on board to stay alive! I know it seems safer, but he will devour you and there will be no salvation as there were for the other three. I can assure you, Captain!" I added as Gavril stormed over. He scrubbed his jaw, taking in the fires burning his ship, the ponderous coils of the serpent squeezing tighter.

"You men, stay aboard!" he roared. "I'll cut you down myself if you abandon us!"

The sailors looked from him to me, then to Agnarr. I spread my hands. "Who are you? Of what people? And what are you called to do?"

"I cannot follow your god," he said.

"Let's not worry about that part yet," I said. "All I want you to do is reclaim who you are."

His eyes bored into mine for a few more moments—gauging my sincerity, I didn't doubt.

"*It is hard for thee to kick against the pricks.* But I cannot force your redemption, I assure you," I said drily. "This is no trap."

Another boom, and the ship lurched. Agnarr gripped the railing, looked around at the sailors gathered. "I am Rolf Kurz. I was born in Kennerdorf, *und ich bin Diutisch!*"

Then serpent roared, its head reeling up from the water. Foam and fire surged as its eyes blazed crimson. It stared at Rolf, then me, then

Thomas. Its teeth bared in rictus, it plunged downward. Rolf's and Thomas' steel met it, driving it off. The coils slacked, but I did not see it diminish in size, or attempt to leave. It brought its head down like a fist again and again, glancing aside as blades flickered toward its eyes.

Why isn't it leaving? What does it still need? Its tail came from behind me, knocking me flat. My head banged off the deck and my vision wavered. I heard Thomas shout, but not what he said. Hands gripped me and hauled me upward and backward. Through the driving rain I saw the terrible head and maw of the Lindwurm falling again and again, swords flashing only faintly in the murk. Maybe if they could put out its eyes? I didn't know. *The truth shall set us free...shall it not?*

My head cleared a little, and I grasped the hands that saved me. "Thank you, Captain," I began, thinking he had been nearest. But when I turned, it was Robert. I studied him as he stared frankly back at me.

"This isn't working," he said finally. "We need the Brothers."

I shook my head minutely. "You are the only Brother we have on board," I said. "What do you say?"

His mouth twisted as he looked aside. Water was sloshing across the deck, though the Lindwurm's fires continued to burn in spite of it. "He's delaying them long enough, distracting them, until we sink," Robert commented, watching Thomas and Rolf fight valiantly, but futilely. He glanced at me. "Your Fire isn't telling you anything?"

I shook my head. "All he told me was of Paul's journey. And there was no serpent in the shipwreck."

Robert leaned back. "Yes there was." When I only stared at him, he continued. "*And when Paul had gathered a bundle of sticks, and laid them on the fire, there came a viper out of the heat, and fastened on his hand. And when the barbarians saw the venomous beast hang on his hand, they said among themselves, No doubt this man is a murderer, whom, though he hath escaped the sea, yet vengeance suffereth not to live. And he shook off the beast into the fire, and felt no harm. Howbeit they looked when he should have swollen, or fallen down dead suddenly: but after they had looked a great while, and saw no harm come to him, they changed their minds, and said that he was a god."*

My eyes widened. I stood and ran toward Thomas and Rolf. "Get out of the way!" I shouted. "Let him bite the ship!"

Rolf moved slower, but Thomas—husband and beloved—knew me well and grabbed Rolf by the arm and dragged him away. The Lindwurm paused only a moment in victory, opened wide his maw and descended. Timbers shattered and the boat shuddered as thunder crashed overhead.

What fire do we shake it off into? I wondered. I saw the fires from his spittle all across the deck, but those were his own, weren't they? Might they not strengthen him?

Except they burned blue. Blue had always been of the Sacred Fire since it came to my hand at the Convent. Blue fire held the castaways not to entrap them, but protecting them until they could be drawn back from the belly of the beast. And the little flames kept the Lindwurm's burning spittle from catching the ship on true fire. *We could not stamp them out, because it is hard indeed to kick against the pricks.* I knelt, plunged my hand into the fires, calling out to Our Father.

With a keening cry the flames rose like a forest of spears. The Lindwurm's glowing red eyes dilated wide, too late, as his great teeth were caught in the timbers of the deck. The sailors had already made sure to avoid the flames, and so were kept safe as the fire like lightning bolted skyward, tearing the Lindwurm to shreds in their flight. They struck the clouds overhead with a terrific thunderclap, and the stormclouds retreated before it. The remains of the serpent rolled overboard, hitting the water with a splash.

I stood shakily, chest heaving. The ship righted itself, the seas calmed, the storm winds ceased to a gentle breeze. As we gaped at each other, one of the sailors suddenly called out: "Port of Algiers, Captain!" He pointed. "Straight ahead."

Chapter 15

As the sailors crowded to the railing in awe and disbelief, I went to Adloth who lay still on the deck. He seemed at peace, as though sleeping normally. I touched his shoulder, felt a brief flicker of the Fire jump into him. He stirred. His eyes fluttered open, roved about. When they lit on me he startled, sitting up as he scrabbled backward away.

"You!" he said, hand outstretched and shaking. "Y-your face…"

I lowered my eyes as my hand went automatically to my scars.

"No, I mean, I know you," he said. "You were there—in the bowels of the snake." I looked up as he studied me earnestly. "You brought me back."

"The Sacred Fire brought you back," I replied. "Through his power were you kept safe, and at the right time he brought you out."

He looked about to protest, but remained silent. He looked up, around, over the railing. "The storm…we're free of it?"

"And Algiers is on the horizon," I affirmed. I rose, dusted off my skirts. They were dry. As I looked around again I took in the ship, whole and sound as though it had sailed in entirely fair weather. The sails bellied in the breeze, the rigging creaking gently and melodically. I shook my head, recalling my own words: *no one will believe you went through such a storm.* What evidence would we have except our own memories?

"How?" Adloth asked.

I looked to him. "Can you stand?" He blinked, placed his palms on the deck, and got up. "I would hear what happened to you inside the serpent," I went on. His color was returning. "Are you hungry? Thirsty?"

"Thirsty, I guess," he said, and wiped his hand across his mouth.

Thomas was already on his way over with a cup from the water barrel. Adloth took it gratefully and drank. He shook his head. "I only vaguely remember leaping off," he said quietly. "It seemed the thing to do, I suppose."

"I am sorry about that," I said quietly.

He glanced up sharply, then his features softened. "Oh, no, not really because of you. I mean, the thought was not foreign to me. But I'm afraid I had said some things to young Ginnie. Encouraged her, perhaps, toward her unwholesome goal."

"How do you know?"

He swallowed. "The serpent," he said. "I could hear him in my thoughts. He was...gloating in how I had helped him mark her. Told me I had sealed her fate, that she would be his unless..." He blinked hard, glancing warily for the serpent to arise again as his voice lowered. "Unless I came in her stead."

"And so you jumped," I breathed, somewhat in awe. I had not marked him as one to sacrifice himself—ungenerously, apparently.

He gave a kind of snorting laugh. "Truth be told, it was not the first precipice I had been tempted to jump off of." He shrugged. "This seemed the most astounding way to go. So I went. And at first it was only cold water, the storm muffled above me. Then I heard a voice calling to me." He grinned wryly. "A siren song, of sorts. When I looked up, his mouth was nearly over me. I had only time to gape, then it was all darkness. I felt little pricks, after that. A bit of a squeeze. Then...nothing, really."

I spared a glance for the torches placed along the railings. Dry. Unlit. Unburnt, even. "Your visage appeared to the rest of us in the flames of the torches," I told him. "You seemed in great agony."

His gaze went distant as the cry of seagulls rose. We must have been drawing nearer the wharf itself. "I guess I was, in a way," he murmured. He focused on me. "I felt like I was in there for an eternity. I thought perhaps I had actually died, and that was the afterlife—simple darkness and silence. I called out for a while, thought maybe I heard some things distantly. At times I swore I heard a far-off boom of thunder, as though a storm still raged across the fields while I was deep inside a house. And...well, I had a lot of time to think. That's when I began to wonder if I was not dead at all. Because I thought over my life, how I had gotten to where I was. I didn't actually re-live it, except maybe as one blind who is simply fed memories. So I could imagine the things, the choices, the people and places, but only in the midst of darkness. And..."

He paused, and I waited some moments. "And what?" I asked finally.

He sighed and looked at me. "And I repented of all of it," he said simply. "In all that darkness and solitude, many of the words you said to me came back, and some I had heard from others, and eventually they became undeniable. And soon I heard that song again, the one that came to me before I was swallowed up."

I frowned. "What did it say?"

"I will lift up mine eyes unto the hills, from whence cometh my help. My help cometh from Our Father, which made heaven and earth." He shook his head. "And yet, when I looked up, it was you. You took my hand, guided me out. Your hand never left mine, and your garments shone brilliant white in the darkness like a beacon. And when I struggled, your hand gripped mine—not hard, but firmly, and I knew even if *I* let go, you would not. The seas roared in—freezing this time, chilling me so I thought my very bones would turn to ice, and my blood pumped slower and slower. And then you spoke to me, words I don't remember, but they brought a flood of warmth and all the ice fled my veins. Sweet and soft you sang something like a lullaby—I think perhaps you did! Somehow, a lullaby from my childhood. And it took me back to my mother's lap. And I slept until you woke me just now."

As he spoke, I blushed, lowering my eyes again. "That was most assuredly the Sacred Fire," I repeated.

"Most assuredly," he agreed. But his voice was soft, and when I looked up, he gazed upon me—not quite in rapture, but certainly a kind of wondering gratitude.

I looked to Thomas, who only folded his arms and cocked an eyebrow playfully. I glared in return, and he smiled. At least he wasn't taking Adloth's fawning words too seriously. "You were aware of no one else while you were there?" I asked instead. He shook his head. "Well. I pray you will have strength to remember your vows once we're in Algiers," I said. He nodded, and I departed. I wondered if Langford and Kingsley had similar experiences.

Both were below again, as the passengers had begun gathering their meager belongings. Thomas and I collected ours as well, amid curious and sometimes grateful glances from the others. Finally, Langford stepped over.

"I heard my goods were thrown overboard after I went," he said.

I looked up hesitantly, but he was smiling. "No fault of yours," he continued hurriedly. "Nor anyone's, I suppose. It had to be done." He bobbed his head. "No captain or crew alive would risk their lives for someone else's cargo."

"What will you do?" I asked.

He sighed. "Oh, I'll send letters to the merchant master. That, too, must be done. I pray only that he will not dispatch assassins."

My brows climbed. "Do you think he will?"

He chuckled. "Perhaps not. But he will need his money back. Perhaps I can make some, somehow, to send with the letter. At the least I can disappear in Algiers until something comes about."

"Not the life you imagined," I said carefully.

His gaze went distant. "No," he said quietly. "But I don't see...I mean, I can't imagine how..."

I smiled grimly. "I think you should try."

His gaze met mine, and I saw his eyes glisten. But he merely nodded, bowed, and turned back to his bags. I glanced aside, saw Charlotte with Kingsley. The twins were awake, alert, but quiet. I studied Ginnie for a moment: she seemed to carry no ill-affects. I made my way over.

"Oh, Rae-Anna," Charlotte said quickly when she spotted me. Kingsley turned, wiped his nose quickly with a kerchief, and cleared his throat.

"Young lady," he said with a bow, his voice deep and quiet. "I am told your Fire saved me."

"From the serpent, yes," I said. "As for the rest..."

He nodded. "Yes. Of course. You understand, fortunes as they are, this journey came with no guarantees—"

I stared at him a moment, then laughed. "Master Kingsley, I expect no guarantees from any earthly source. But I hope you understand I came with my own."

"Of course, of course," he said quickly. "I've thanked you for that. But I just meant—well, I know your passage was not free. None is. But, if you were hoping—"

"Master Kingsley," I interrupted before he made himself too crass for honor. "As I said, I came with my own assurances. And, as you have seen, we've arrived in Algiers with our ship and our lives intact. Do you think I ask for more than that?"

He cleared his throat again. "No. Of course not. Forgive me, but others have suggested...well, never mind. Good day to you." He shuffled past in the tight quarters, glanced back saying, "Forgive me," once more before moving to the hatch.

I smiled and turned back to Charlotte, who looked stricken. "Do forgive him," she said quietly. "For...well, everything. Perhaps he should have stayed..." She cut herself off with a tight smile as she kissed the tops of the twins' heads.

I smiled at Ginnie. "How are you, little one?" I asked.

She folded her arms as she frowned. "I'm not little," she said. But her smile quickly overcame her, and she giggled behind her hand. I laughed too. There were no marks or remnants of scales on her skin anywhere I could see, and she definitely possessed a child-like quality, now. Charlotte paled a moment before smiling beatifically upon her 'eldest' daughter.

"Are you staying in Algiers?" I asked. My assumption was they would go where the boat did, but after that experience...

She nodded. "Not for the reason you might assume—I assumed, even, when daddy told me. But he intends to refit the ship to match his original design. He assures me the sailors have already made inspections, and every seam and timber is sound. He said, though," she added with a wry smile, "that it is as weathered as a ship with fifty voyages behind it."

I cocked my head. "Which would mean it's as seaworthy as any ship can be, wouldn't it?"

She grinned. "You have a sailor's mind already, as well—perhaps you are as seaworthy now as any sailor could be. But yes, it is the finest vessel daddy ever made." She glanced behind me to where Thomas still sat with our things. "What about you? Do you know yet what brought you here?"

I took a breath to seek the Fire, confirm some things that had come to us during the trip. "It is too soon to be certain," I said, feeling no sharpness in the prompting. "But I think we know where to start."

"But...I mean, you will not live here."

I grinned. *"If Our Father will, we shall live, and do this, or that,"* I said. "Some of our appointments have been a few weeks. In Fosse we were permitted to stay the winter."

"I see. Well, if it is permitted, we will take you back across when it is time." She smiled. "I would love to have you on board again."

I cocked an eyebrow. "Not just for fighting off sea serpents, I hope?"

She laughed. "No, of course not. But I'm afraid I did not get to know you as well as I would have liked."

I shrugged. "Perhaps during times of testing, we get to know each other far better than times of peace. But I know what you mean," I said quickly. "I would not mind that, at all. And yet." I paused as the Fire flickered, and my grin faded. I regarded her concerned gaze, forced a smile back to my lips. "Well, there are many excellent people in the world to befriend. My journey is yet long and circuitous." I laid a hand on her arm as her fingers pressed to her mouth. "Remain firm in Our Father, and we will have an eternity to praise Him. And I daresay you have your own journey before you?"

Her lips quirked. "I suppose I have."

I looked earnestly at her. "Do not suppose: you do. And if not as peculiar as mine, it is singular, and full of its own joys and triumphs. Lean into those, seek the beauty in it, the wonder and awe. And if you remember me it will be fondly, not in sorrow. As I will remember you."

She nodded, drawing Ginnie and Jonnie tight to her again. I blessed them all and turned away to see Robert watching me. I waggled my eyebrows: nowhere to escape on a ship. I returned to my hammock, drawing some strength from Thomas' admiring gaze. "What?" I asked him quietly.

But he only pursed his lips and shook his head, his smile playful. And with secret promise. I rolled my eyes mockingly, then looked up quickly as Robert came forward. "Forgive me," I began, but his raised hand halted me.

"You have it, of course—what you need. But... I judged you, both of you, most harshly. And never more harshly than as the journey progressed. But your words at the end, there." He shook his head. "Well. I cannot think of anyone of more grace than you had, especially with all that was happening. Not even I—"

This time I cut him off with a raised hand. "Our Father provides each of us what we need for our journey on this earth, according to his discretion and purposes. *Now there are diversities of gifts, but the same Sacred Fire. But the manifestation of the Sacred Fire is given to every man to profit withal. But all these worketh that one and the selfsame Sacred Fire, dividing to every man severally as he will.*"

His smile was tight. "That still doesn't bode much hope for me. If this is to become part of my journey..."

"It may not. Perhaps this was merely an intersection. Take what you can from it, and look to the road laid out in front of you." I paused as he cast his eyes downward. "Do you know what road the Brothers of Chantereaux laid out for you?" I asked.

He drew a heavy sigh. "Now you mention them…they do not exist."

I waited with wide eyes for his explanation.

"I thought to minister to the tribes in Ifriqiya," he murmured. "The Brothers in Morlaigne said I should not, so I told them I already had a blessing from Chantereaux. So they blessed me as well, and gave me fare for the ship." When he glanced up his eyes glistened. "Perhaps they were right, though."

"Did you think such an undertaking would be without opposition?" I asked. He studied me, but was silent. "I can assure you, my introduction to the war of the Sacred Fire was no less precipitous than this may be for you," I continued with a grin. "Or did you suppose he bestowed his gifts just so you might not be angry when someone annoys you? You've heard of his power, I don't doubt, from the Brothers. Now you have seen it at work on the seas. Such great power does not exist without opposition to match it. Oh, the Liar is defeated, I know," I said as he opened his mouth to protest. "And yet *your adversary the Liar, as a roaring lion, walketh about, seeking whom he may devour.* You may come to understand this analogy intimately, if you continue into the interior of the continent. I hear lions roam about, roaring, all over the place here."

He smiled appreciatively. "Yes, I suppose that's true. It's easy, amid such comfort, to take the battles of the unseen realm lightly."

I laughed. "Many have discovered so. Would that they knew how we on the front lines of it fared or struggled."

He shrugged. "Perhaps not. As in any war, those on the front lines fight precisely so those at home are blissfully unaware."

I hummed. "We both know the Liar respects no battle lines, though."

He nodded soberly. "Indeed. Well, perhaps I will recruit more to our fight, then."

"I will remember you in my prayers," I promised.

"And I, you," he responded. "And will tell of you to any of the Brothers I meet along the way."

I grinned. "I would appreciate that a lot," I said.

He bowed and departed. I glanced back to Thomas, but saw he had also left while I was distracted. I frowned—how had I missed that? I turned back for the hatch, nearly running into Agnarr—Rolf, as he stood as if waiting for me. I looked warily at him, wondering if the change had stuck, or if it was made in haste and under duress. He studied me with his sapphire eyes, and a grin relaxed his features. I was glad to see it back.

"And what of you?" I asked, almost mechanically. It was quickly becoming a habit to check in with everyone. I half expected to talk with every sailor on my way to the dock. And where *had* Thomas gone?

"I wanted to stay with you two for a little longer," he said, almost shyly.

I blinked. It did not fit with one of his stature, that shyness. "Oh?" was all I could muster.

"Will that cause pain?" he asked.

I frowned. "Pain? I would hope not—"

He waved his hands dismissively. "I mean, it will not upset you if I do?"

"Oh! No, I don't think so. I'm just curious why, I suppose."

His fists clenched and unclenched. "You spoke truth. I left my *dorf* promising to find what I needed to come back and defeat our enemy. It *is* an old evil, but it is no creature. It attacks our crops, poisons our water. Our children die in the night, and our men are too weak to work. My people looked to me, who had begun to follow the old gods, to go on quest to find the old cure."

My eyes widened. "And it's in Ifriqiya?" I asked.

When his face fell, I suddenly suspected the truth. I let him say it, though. "Your Brother Robert has told me some of the tale of Jonah. And I am doing what he did—was doing it, anyway. Running away. I had intended never to return. They would think I had died," he went on, shrugging. "Another would have been sent, and perhaps would have completed the quest. Either way, I had no longer wanted that life."

"And yet you delay returning," I said cautiously.

His eyes brightened. "As I said, you spoke truly: the hero was to be me. But I also spoke truly: I was told privately I would find what I seek in the land of the dark-skinned. A warrior who would come as a sacrifice, but escape with grace."

I swallowed, remembering the prophecy he had told, and Thomas' connection with The Beloved as the Lamb. But had Rolf figured out its meaning? He smiled gently as he watched my face. I squared my shoulders. "You know who it is?" I asked.

"I suspected by your reaction earlier. But by your reaction just now, you made it plain. And it has to do with your name, does it not?"

I sighed and nodded. "Rae-Anna comes from a name meaning 'Lamb of Grace,'" I said. "At least, as far as I was told."

His smile widened until teeth showed. "All right then." He jerked his head toward the hatch. "Let's go ashore."

Chapter 16

THOMAS

As Rae-Anna spoke with Robert, I felt the Seed stirring in me, calling me topside. As soon as my eyes cleared the hatchway, I saw Mahmoud facing the shore, his arms folded tightly. Khalid was moving away, and somehow I could tell they had just finished speaking. And the topic was not pleasant.

I climbed the rest of the way out and made my way over. "Mahmoud?" I asked as I neared.

The only indication he heard me was a slight twitch in his shoulder. I moved up beside him, watching the docks sliding slowly nearer. Sailors and dock workers swarmed the shore, the buildings behind it brilliantly white in the sunlight. Already, the noise of the port rolled across the sea, a cacophony of voices, most of which I couldn't understand. I checked a sigh: if The Beloved brought us here, it was for a reason. And, at least for now, we had a guide.

"I've not been to such a big city," I murmured.

He relaxed minutely as he glanced at me. "We will not stay in it for long."

"Oh? I thought you had business..." I trailed off as the thought struck me. "Or, do you mean since we lost all our cargo?"

He shook his head. "No, there is no harm. That was surplus. But my father is outside the city. If you are staying with me," he added, cocking an eyebrow, "you will live as a *badawi*. He prefers the old ways, still." He went silent, his dark eyes taking in the docks. I thought I could tell which one the captain was making for, saw a few workers starting to get to their feet to receive us. Mahmoud sighed shortly, half-turning. He hesitated, then said: "Forgive me, Thomas, for what I am about to do to you."

I froze, gripped the Seed as if to pry it open for some sort of power or help. But it merely warmed, and I felt a peaceful breeze through me, carrying away my apprehension. "How so?" I asked, more lightly than I still felt.

"You had a time of peace and plenty in Fosse. I had hoped...prayed, to Allah," he added awkwardly. The fact it seemed an afterthought struck me, but I didn't pursue it. "Prayed that we would get there in winter, knowing we would be held there until spring. After leaving you in Aurden..." He pressed his lips together, shook his head. "For that, too, I ask forgiveness. I thought you would come to your senses there, to abandon this *Jeshua,* this Beloved you claim. I did not realize the danger, truly," he went on, turning toward me with an earnestness I had never seen in him before. "I had hoped to come back, offer you the peace of Allah, and go on. When I saw Rae-Anna's face..." He swallowed hard, turned resolutely back to the sea. After some moments—during which, I admit, I gripped the Seed even tighter to keep my physical fingers from gripping Mahmoud's neck—he seemed to master himself. "I have treated the one who healed me with utter contempt. Risked her life to prove a point."

"Mahmoud," I interrupted quickly. Now I had found firm footing again. "I believe she has told you, and I repeat it: her life is in no one's hands but The Beloved's. Any risk to her life is brought through him, not you or anyone else."

He lowered his gaze a moment, then brought it back up. "I believe she did say something similar, once. 'What you meant for evil…'?"

I smiled grimly. *"But as for you, ye thought evil against me; but Our Father meant it unto good, to bring to pass, as it is this day, to save much people alive,"* I said. "Without His presence there through us, Aurden would still be full of living dead, enslaved by an ancient demon and multiple foul spirits."

He swallowed again. "Yes, that is what she said." He drew a deep breath and blew it out. "So when we came to Fosse, I hoped to balance what I did by taking us somewhere to find much rest." He turned again to me. "I swear I did not know about the dragon, or the dangers of that place—"

"Mahmoud, I will say it again: Our Father is taking us on a journey of His design. We will face dangers everywhere we go, I do not doubt. Whatever your intentions, that will not change."

He considered me a moment, eyes glittering. "Do my intentions matter?" he asked.

"Ah," I said with a nod. "Yes, they do. In part."

"What part?"

I smiled. "Well, on the one hand, *He that receiveth you receiveth me, and he that receiveth me receiveth him that sent me. And whosoever shall give to drink unto one of these little ones a cup of cold water only in the name of a disciple, verily I say unto you, he shall in no wise lose his reward."*

"And what is the other part?"

My grin slipped, and I returned his gaze steadily. *"For they that are after the flesh do mind the things of the flesh; but they that are after the*

Sacred Fire the things of the Sacred Fire. Because the carnal mind is enmity against Our Father: for it is not subject to the law of Our Father, neither indeed can be. So then they that are in the flesh cannot please Our Father. However," I went on, "I believe a heart is softened by the first part, so that it will not continue in enmity as deeply as if it continues to do harm. And the fact that you are so repentant of your intentions at Aurden gives me hope that I am right."

He stared at me some time longer, then turned away again as his eyes cast over the shoreline of his homeland. "Last year I would have taken offense that you think I would turn from the God of my fathers," he said. "As I return home now, it disturbs me that your words give me...hope." He pressed his lips together as his gaze fell again.

I let the silence draw on for a space. A thought struck me, a suggestion from the Seed, and I drew another breath. "Is that what you and Khalid have been arguing about?"

He frowned, cast me a quick glance. "Yes," he said. "Khalid has been warning me about wandering from my faith. I have tried to defend you and Rae-Anna." He paused and eyed me. "Defend you, not your faith. I hope you understand." I nodded and he went on after a deep breath. "Khalid has not seen what I have seen. And he has always been more...zealous for the faith than I have."

I squinted. "Didn't you say he has divers weights in his pack?"

Mahmoud snorted. "As well as in his mind—always weighing others with more precise weights than he does himself."

I couldn't help but grin. "The Beloved spoke about that as well. I think that's a very human thing to do."

He nodded begrudgingly. "Perhaps you are right. But Khalid is furious, now, knowing that you two still live and will be going to my father's tent with me."

"That matters to him?"

"As I said, he is most zealous."

I frowned, shaking my head. "Forgive me, that still doesn't make sense…" I looked up suddenly. "You never told me what you are about to do with us, that we need to forgive you."

He studied me. "Do you distrust me?"

My jaw flapped once. "I mean, I guess not. I believe you that you intended to give us rest at Fosse. And, obviously, you couldn't know what perils lay on this voyage." I gave a quick nod of confirmation. "So I guess I believe you are not actively seeking to harm us."

He gave the faintest of grins. "I have earned as much, I suppose." He turned shoreward again, and I stared at him as the silence dragged on.

Finally, I blurted: "But what are you about to do to us?"

"I am taking you where you are unwelcome," he said simply. "In the name of trade, I could perhaps bring you. Alone. You would be given the barest hospitality, the greatest of distrust, and I could not promise favorable dealings until you had been proven."

"But we're not trading," I said.

He shook his head. "No. I bring you, through whom your Father is constantly at work, who may threaten my family's worship and faith. And I bring both of you, for I do not believe Rae-Anna would stay in the city." He glanced at me, and I shook my head: she absolutely would not, if The Beloved was leading us to Mahmoud's tents. And both our prayers pointed us that direction. He read all that, I believe, in my eyes. And he nodded curtly. "So I must bring two of you, against all wisdom. Then, with no promises of good faith, I will take you again into known danger, and all to help me." He shook his head. "At least I do not bring *three* infidels," he muttered.

I tried to ignore his comment, despite a warm chuckle from the

Seed. "What help do you need?"

"Khalid," he said heavily. "His threat during the storm was not empty. He intends to bring charges against me, and to see me beheaded. For failing the faith, and for dealing so closely with you, and whatever else he can bring."

"But will we be able to defend you? I can't imagine they would listen to us, given what you just said."

His jaw worked a few times as he ground his teeth together. "Perhaps not. Perhaps your Father will…"

"You think Khalid is demonic? That seems to be the cause of all of our battles so far."

"I do not know. I thought, perhaps…"

"Maybe if Our Father would do this for you, you would follow Him?"

His eyes flashed, then dropped in shame. "Forgive me. It is foolish. Forget I asked—"

I held up a hand to stop him. "Let's not fetter Our Father—one way or another. Maybe He will do this for you. Maybe He will do something even greater. But you know by now: He will work as He wills, and Rae-Anna and I can only be His instruments."

"Even though I lead you into danger again?" he asked.

"Mahmoud, have you been listening?" I chided with a grin. "Our Father leads us, not you. I can assure you, if it were not His will, I would not be promising to go with you. Know for certain I would not put Rae-Anna in danger if I thought for a moment Our Father would not be with us."

He considered that a moment, then cocked an eyebrow. "By that reasoning, Thomas, you say it is Your Father's will to help me. That He is already listening to me."

"I would consider the possibility, Mahmoud, that you are already listening to Him—that it is He who brings you along this path, not you who has been granted a favor. The Last Apostle was on his way to destroy those of the faith, and on that exact road was where The Beloved met him."

By now the ship was approaching the dock, and boats had come out to guide us alongside it. Lines shot from the deck by the sailors and were quickly tied off. The gangplank was run out as the rest of the passengers began milling near the railing.

"Thomas!" Rae-Anna called suddenly. I looked back and saw her emerging from the hatch. As her feet cleared the last rung, I saw Rolf's head bobbing into view. "There you are. I hope you don't mind: Rolf is coming with us too."

I felt Mahmoud tense, but didn't dare look at him. "Is he?" I asked.

She nodded, smiling. There was a hesitancy to it, but I didn't want to press it right then. "He has more work to find his hero—that is, what his village needs. It's a cure of some kind, apparently. And I think he'll find it if he's with us."

I glanced at Mahmoud, then, saw his eyes glittering darkly and with no small amount of fear. And I'm afraid I didn't have any words for him that would help him understand. I would continue to leave it, apparently, for Our Father.

Ah, Father, who speaks words fitly for each person according to their need. How we would come to rely on His words in the land of the Arab and the Moor.

Scripture References

Chapter 2:

"Let no man despise thy youth; but be thou an example of the believers, in word, in conversation, in charity, in spirit, in faith, in purity." 1Ti 4:12

"They that go down to the sea in ships, that do business in great waters; 24 These see the works of the LORD, and his wonders in the deep." Psa 107:23-24

"Then they cry unto the LORD in their trouble, and he bringeth them out of their distresses. 29 He maketh the storm a calm, so that the waves thereof are still. 30 Then are they glad because they be quiet; so he bringeth them unto their desired haven." Psa 107:28-30

Chapter 3:

"Therefore all things whatsoever ye would that men should do to you, do ye even so to them: for this is the law and the prophets." Mat 7:12

"But Jonah rose up to flee unto Tarshish from the presence of the LORD, and went down to Joppa; and he found a ship going to Tarshish: so he paid the fare thereof, and went down into it, to go with them unto Tarshish from the presence of the LORD. 4 But the LORD sent out a great wind into the sea, and there was a mighty tempest in the sea, so that the ship was like to be broken." Jon 1:3-4

Chapter 5:

"Thou shalt not have in thy bag divers weights, a great and a small. 14 Thou shalt not have in thine house divers measures, a great and a small. ... 16 For all that do such things, [and] all that do unrighteously, [are] an abomination unto the LORD thy God." Deu 25:13-14, 16

"Paul said to the centurion and to the soldiers, Except these abide in the ship, ye cannot be saved." Act 27:31

"The LORD [is] good unto them that wait for him, to the soul [that] seeketh him." Lam 3:25

"The Lord is not slack concerning his promise, as some men count slackness; but is longsuffering to us-ward, not willing that any should perish, but that all should come to repentance." 2Pe 3:9

"And they were all amazed, insomuch that they questioned among themselves, saying, What thing is this? what new doctrine [is] this? for with authority commandeth he even the unclean spirits, and they do obey him." Mar 1:27

Chapter 6:

"Canst thou draw out leviathan with an hook? or his tongue with a cord [which] thou lettest down? 2 Canst thou put an hook into his nose? or bore his jaw through with a thorn?" Job 41:1-2

"But whoso shall offend one of these little ones which believe in me, it were better for him that a millstone were hanged about his neck, and [that] he were drowned in the depth of the sea." Mat 18:6

"The one who eats everything must not treat with contempt the one who does not, and the one who does not eat everything must not judge the one who does, for God has accepted them." Rom 14:3

Chapter 7:

"But thus saith the LORD, Even the captives of the mighty shall be taken away, and the prey of the terrible shall be delivered: for I will contend with him that contendeth with thee, and I will save thy children." Isa 49:25

"Surely he hath borne our griefs, and carried our sorrows: yet we did esteem him stricken, smitten of God, and afflicted. 5 But he [was] wounded for our transgressions, [he was] bruised for our iniquities: the chastisement of our peace [was] upon him; and with his stripes we are healed." Isa 53:4-5

"The light of the body is the eye: if therefore thine eye be single, thy whole body shall be full of light." Mat 6:22

"God [is] not a man, that he should lie; neither the son of man, that he should repent: hath he said, and shall he not do [it]? or hath he spoken, and shall he not make it good?" Num 23:19

"They that go down to the sea in ships, that do business in great waters; 24 These see the works of the LORD, and his wonders in the deep. 25 For he commandeth, and raiseth the stormy wind, which lifteth up the waves thereof. 26 They mount up to the heaven, they go down again to the depths: their soul is melted because of trouble. 27 They reel to and fro, and stagger like a drunken man, and are at their wits' end. 28 Then they cry unto the LORD in their trouble, and he bringeth them out of their distresses." Psa 107:23-28

Chapter 8:

"And said, I cried by reason of mine affliction unto the LORD, and he heard me; out of the belly of hell cried I, [and] thou heardest my voice." Jon 2:2

"The waters compassed me about, [even] to the soul: the depth closed me round about, the weeds were wrapped about my head. 6 I went down to the bottoms of the mountains; the earth with her bars [was] about me for ever: yet hast thou brought up my life from corruption, O LORD my God." Jon 2:5-6

"When my soul fainted within me I remembered the LORD: and my prayer came in unto thee, into thine holy temple. ...4 Then I said, I am cast out of thy sight; yet I will look again toward thy holy temple." Jon 2:7, 4

"And when he sowed, some [seeds] fell by the way side, and the fowls came and devoured them up:" Mat 13:4

"Then Peter and the [other] apostles answered and said, We ought to obey God rather than men." Act 5:29

"Jesus answered and said unto them, Ye do err, not knowing the scriptures, nor the power of God." Mat 22:29

"But the heavens and the earth, which are now, by the same word are kept in store, reserved unto fire against the day of judgment and perdition of ungodly men. ... 9 The Lord is not slack concerning his promise, as some men count slackness; but is longsuffering to us-ward, not willing that any should perish, but that all should come to repentance." 2Pe 3:7, 9

"And Adam gave names to all cattle, and to the fowl of the air, and to every beast of the field; but for Adam there was not found an help meet for him. ... 22 And the rib, which the LORD God had taken from man, made he a woman, and brought her unto the man. ... 24 Therefore shall a man leave his father and his mother, and shall cleave unto his wife: and they shall be one flesh." Gen 2:20, 22, 24

"Let no man say when he is tempted, I am tempted of God: for God cannot be tempted with evil, neither tempteth he any man." Jas 1:13

"God [is] not a man, that he should lie; neither the son of man, that he should repent: hath he said, and shall he not do [it]? or hath he spoken, and shall he not make it good?" Num 23:19

"(For we walk by faith, not by sight:)" 2Co 5:7

"Now when they saw the boldness of Peter and John, and perceived that they were unlearned and ignorant men, they marvelled; and they took knowledge of them, that they had been with Jesus." Act 4:13

"And he said unto them, Come ye yourselves apart into a desert place, and rest a while: for there were many coming and going, and they had no leisure so much as to eat." Mar 6:31

Chapter 9:

"Not that I speak in respect of want: for I have learned, in whatsoever state I am, [therewith] to be content." Phl 4:11

"For we which live are alway delivered unto death for Jesus' sake, that the life also of Jesus might be made manifest in our mortal flesh." 2Co 4:11

"That ye may with one mind [and] one mouth glorify God, even the Father of our Lord Jesus Christ." Rom 15:6

Chapter 10:

"Every branch in me that beareth not fruit he taketh away: and every [branch] that beareth fruit, he purgeth it, that it may bring forth more fruit." Jhn 15:2

"How beautiful upon the mountains are the feet of him that bringeth good tidings, that publisheth peace; that bringeth good tidings of good, that publisheth salvation; that saith unto Zion, Thy God reigneth!" Isa 52:7

"And the king of Israel said unto Jehoshaphat, [There is] yet one man, Micaiah the son of Imlah, by whom we may enquire of the LORD: but I hate him; for he doth not prophesy good concerning me, but evil. And Jehoshaphat said, Let not the king say so." 1Ki 22:8

"There hath no temptation taken you but such as is common to man: but God [is] faithful, who will not suffer you to be tempted above that ye are able; but will with the temptation also make a way to escape, that ye may be able to bear [it]." 1Co 10:13

Chapter 11:

"Or [who] shut up the sea with doors, when it brake forth, [as if] it had issued out of the womb? ... 10 And brake up for it my decreed [place], and set bars and doors, 11 And said, Hitherto shalt thou come, but no further: and here shall thy proud waves be stayed?" Job 38:8, 10-11

"For he commandeth, and raiseth the stormy wind, which lifteth up the waves thereof." Psa 107:25

Chapter 12:

"Because strait [is] the gate, and narrow [is] the way, which leadeth unto life, and few there be that find it." Mat 7:14

"Not that I speak in respect of want: for I have learned, in whatsoever state I am, [therewith] to be content." Phl 4:11

"And the LORD God commanded the man, saying, Of every tree of the garden thou mayest freely eat:" Gen 2:16

"Whatsoever thy hand findeth to do, do [it] with thy might; for [there is] no work, nor device, nor knowledge, nor wisdom, in the grave, whither thou goest." Ecc 9:10

"Whether therefore ye eat, or drink, or whatsoever ye do, do all to the glory of God." 1Co 10:31

"And all things, whatsoever ye shall ask in prayer, believing, ye shall receive." Mat 21:22

"Thou shalt tread upon the lion and adder: the young lion and the dragon shalt thou trample under feet." Psa 91:13

"And he joined himself with him to make ships to go to Tarshish: and they made the ships in Eziongeber. 37 Then Eliezer the son of Dodavah of Mareshah prophesied against Jehoshaphat, saying, Because thou hast joined thyself with Ahaziah, the LORD hath broken thy works. And the ships were broken, that they were not able to go to Tarshish." 2Ch 20:36-37

Chapter 13:

"Remember ye not the former things, neither consider the things of old." Isa 43:18

"How then shall they call on him in whom they have not believed? and how shall they believe in him of whom they have not heard? and how shall they hear without a preacher?" Rom 10:14

"The Lord is not slack concerning his promise, as some men count slackness; but is longsuffering to us-ward, not willing that any should perish, but that all should come to repentance." 2Pe 3:9

"O Jerusalem, Jerusalem, [thou] that killest the prophets, and stonest them which are sent unto thee, how often would I have gathered thy children together, even as a hen gathereth her chickens under [her] wings, and ye would not!" Mat 23:37

"And the lord said unto the servant, Go out into the highways and hedges, and compel [them] to come in, that my house may be filled." Luk 14:23

"And he said unto him, If they hear not Moses and the prophets, neither will they be persuaded, though one rose from the dead." Luk 16:31

"They have seen vanity and lying divination, saying, The LORD saith: and the LORD hath not sent them: and they have made [others] to hope that they would confirm the word. ... 8 Therefore thus saith the Lord GOD; Because ye have spoken vanity, and seen lies, therefore, behold, I [am] against you, saith the Lord GOD. 9 And mine hand shall be upon the prophets that see vanity, and that divine lies: they shall not be in the assembly of my people, neither shall they be written in the writing of the house of Israel, neither shall they enter into the land of Israel; and ye shall know that I [am] the Lord GOD." Eze 13:6, 8-9

"If we confess our sins, he is faithful and just to forgive us [our] sins, and to cleanse us from all unrighteousness. 10 If we say that we have not sinned, we make him a liar, and his word is not in us." 1Jo 1:9-10

Chapter 14:

"Above all, taking the shield of faith, wherewith ye shall be able to quench all the fiery darts of the wicked." Eph 6:16

"The heavens declare the glory of God; and the firmament sheweth his handywork. 2 Day unto day uttereth speech, and night unto night sheweth knowledge. 3 [There is] no speech nor language, [where] their voice is not heard. 4 Their line is gone out through all the earth, and their words to the end of the world. In them hath he set a tabernacle for the sun," Psa 19:1-4

"For they that are after the flesh do mind the things of the flesh; but they that are after the Spirit the things of the Spirit." Rom 8:5

"And when Paul had gathered a bundle of sticks, and laid [them] on the fire, there came a viper out of the heat, and fastened on his hand. 4 And when the barbarians saw the [venomous] beast hang on his hand, they said among themselves, No doubt this man is a murderer, whom, though he hath escaped the sea, yet vengeance suffereth not to live. 5 And he shook off the beast into the fire, and felt no harm. 6 Howbeit they looked when he should have swollen, or fallen down dead suddenly: but after they had looked a great while, and saw no harm come to him, they changed their minds, and said that he was a god." Act 28:3-6

Chapter 15:

"I will lift up mine eyes unto the hills, from whence cometh my help. 2 My help [cometh] from the LORD, which made heaven and earth." Psa 121:1-2

"For that ye [ought] to say, If the Lord will, we shall live, and do this, or that." Jas 4:15

"Now there are diversities of gifts, but the same Spirit. ... 7 But the manifestation of the Spirit is given to every man to profit withal. ... 11 But all these worketh that one and the selfsame Spirit, dividing to every man severally as he will." 1Co 12:4, 7, 11

"Be sober, be vigilant; because your adversary the devil, as a roaring lion, walketh about, seeking whom he may devour:" 1Pe 5:8

Chapter 16:

"But as for you, ye thought evil against me; [but] God meant it unto good, to bring to pass, as [it is] this day, to save much people alive." Gen 50:20

"He that receiveth you receiveth me, and he that receiveth me receiveth him that sent me. ... 42 And whosoever shall give to drink unto one of these little ones a cup of cold [water] only in the name of a disciple, verily I say unto you, he shall in no wise lose his reward." Mat 10:40, 42

"For they that are after the flesh do mind the things of the flesh;

but they that are after the Spirit the things of the Spirit. ... 7 Because the carnal mind [is] enmity against God: for it is not subject to the law of God, neither indeed can be. 8 So then they that are in the flesh cannot please God." Rom 8:5, 7-8

"And when we were all fallen to the earth, I heard a voice speaking unto me, and saying in the Hebrew tongue, Saul, Saul, why persecutest thou me? [it is] hard for thee to kick against the pricks." Act 26:14

About the Author

Daniel Dydek is an Iraq-war veteran, and multi-genre author. His writings include his sweeping epic fantasy series The Triumvirs; and his supernatural suspense series, Spirit Wind, has already garnered two Finalist awards from Realm Makers. Besides writing, he also enjoys a personal relationship with Jesus Christ, mountain biking, reading, coffee shops, book stores, and Durango Colorado. He lives in Canton Ohio with his wife and son and two cats.

Support for the Author

First, thank you for reading this story on whichever medium you chose—Kindle, KU, or paperback. Your support means dreams come true! If you loved the story, there are a lot of ways to continue supporting the author FOR FREE. Here's a few:

1. Subscribe to the newsletter on danieldydek.com

2. Tell your friends!

3. Leave a review on Goodreads, Amazon, Barnes & Noble, or on your social media. (This is probably the greatest support of all, because we love hearing what people enjoyed about the book! Plus, you know, algorithms...)

4. Ask your local library to get a copy

All these things help promote the books, and encourage the author to keep writing stories you'll love!

—The Beorn Publishing Team

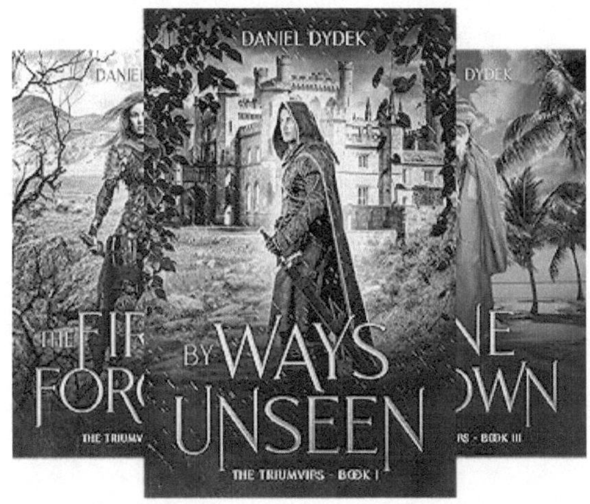

Centuries ago, the world of Oren was ravaged by uncontrolled magic during the Wizards War. In the wake of such devastation and evil, the God of All took three wizards and established for them a Room, of darkness and consciousness, and placed before them a great table whose appearance is of translucent slate, through which they might call up visions of the lands, entering when needed. Few even know these former wizards exist, and their work will always be credited to brave men and women of the world who were faithful in their obedience.

These wizards' task is keeping the peace, of prompting action against the forces of evil. They answer still to the God of All, but retain autonomy. He named them The Triumvirate, and over the centuries twenty-two Triumvirs have guided Oren through wars, famines, pestilences, and the rising and falling of countless empires.

Now, in this current Age of men, will come their most difficult battle.

Amazon search: The Triumvirs Dydek

www.ingramcontent.com/pod-product-compliance
Lightning Source LLC
Chambersburg PA
CBHW060542160726
47991CB00001B/420